MAGNIFICENT REVEAL

BY RAYNER TAPIA

Strategic Book Publishing and Rights Co.

Strategic Book Publishing and Rights Co., LLC
USA | Singapore
www.sbpra.com

For information about special discounts for bulk purchases, please contact Strategic Book Publishing and Rights Co., LLC Special Sales, at bookorder@sbpra.net.

ISBN: 978-1-948260-29-9

In your memory, Dad.
Miss you every day.

For Mum and my sisters, love you forever.

CONTENTS

ACKNOWLEDGEMENTS

 To the wonderful people I have met during the creation and writing of my fifth instalment. Thank you all so much.

The encouragement you gave me inspired me to write even more.

Thank you to my dear friends for your support and belief. There are so many to name. Here are just a few: Chamber of Commerce NWL, President Carole Marblestein, Mr. Lewis Evans — magical music composer to accompany books, Rowena, Shelley, Carina, Derrick.

The JS team: Elaine, Sarah, Pravina, Chreen, Hetal, Anita, Hassan, Nandini, Kanye, Alex (*Goose*), and John. Thank you all for your kind support and help every time. You all gave me courage.

Fahima, Shelma, Sally, Saher, Evelina, Martha, Dominica, Valerie, Maseema, Marilyn, Vanessa, Helen, Mandy, Carina Rawlings, Ruth, Diane B., Sue Ward, David, Christine, Maria, Nathalie, Milo, and Mr. George Ruddock for your ineffable, ongoing support. Thank you all so much.

To my dear family, who supported me and tolerated my moments during the creation and writing of my new book. Thank you ever so much more.

MAGNIFICENT REVEAL

SYNOPSIS

James embarks on a journey to bring his brother back to planet Earth. He aims to stop the powerful demon Morkann in her malevolent ambitions. He invites his feisty scientist friend Amber Rawlings to accompany him. Together, they reach the strange lands through the Milky Way. They meet many magnificent creatures crossing unforeseen lands where good and evil forces commence battle.

OBLIVIONARA

MOUNTAINS OF
THE MOON

GRIMMS
MARSH

BOILER
ROOM

WISHING
WELL

RIPPLE MARSH

OLD
OAK TREE

ORACLE

PALACE
OF GREATNESS

CLOMP OF
TUMBLEWOOD

COURT OF
PRYTONEUM

DEMON ORACLE

MARSHES

TOWER OF
BELLE À NOIR

MORIADIYA

CHAPTER 1

THE RETURN

It had been a year since James had left his brother Tom on the blazing gorge that had separated them as its ferocious flames raged through the rocks. He tried in desperation to cling onto Tom, but his grip faltered, and he was forced by Nataliya, the Labyrinth of Light, to let go and save himself from the raging flames. James watched the shadows of his brother and of Nataliya disappear into the distance, sensing he would never see them again.

The months came and went. James lived his life without his brother; however, James often wondered about Tom and if he had survived and if he would ever see him again.

The afternoon came to a close, and James watched

the old clock tick past through the hour. Suddenly, a blaring phone shattered the silence. He looked down the hallway, where a short, sharp trill echoed through the barren walls. Lost in deep thought the ringing seemed to beckon him into the drawing room, so he paced slowly through the door and then rushed towards the hallway where the phone blared loudly. He hoped it was a call to lure him back to the planets, just like he hoped for most nights, endlessly waiting for that call. The right moment had to come to search for his family. James, not knowing what he was in search of, maybe a clue, anything, someone, something that would take him back to the worlds where he had lost his brother and his mother.

The phone continued to ring louder and louder, reverberating through the house. He finally seized the receiver. He wanted to hear someone, a sign that would lead him once again to his brother Tom. This was how James spent his days and nights, just hoping for a connection. He always anticipated he would find that connection, but when it would come, he did not know.

"Hello," James answered anxiously, his piercing, ocean-blue eyes wide and waiting.

After a slight pause, a voice replied excitedly, "Hi, James, it's me, Amber. Just wanted to know how you were today?"

"Oh, Amber, it's you. I am doing well."

"Uh-huh, doing well," Amber repeated sarcastically. "Literally that means, not good. Don't ask," she snapped. "Listen, I know something that may cheer you up. The Space Agency is running a test run on the heath tomorrow. I thought we could take a ride in their shuttle to explore space. Should be good. What do you think? We could find your planets."

"No, I don't think so," James replied, smiling to himself.

"James, you said your brother was lost in space. So, we can find him, right?"

"We! What do you mean, *we*? Are you mad or just carrying out one of your experiments?" replied a startled James.

Although James was keen to participate in Amber's wild escapades, he had no idea about the Space Agency test run, but he was aware of Amber's scientific knowledge, realising she would be an intelligent and much-needed travel companion if she were to accompany him to the planets. However, would he? Could he entrust her with knowing his mother was an alien, let alone the life forms he had discovered, along with his brother remaining on the planet. His mind was awash with dilemmas, turmoil, and much confusion, which etched upon his face like the wrinkles of an old man.

Amber Rawlings had smooth, olive-coloured skin. She was tall and slim with raven, silky hair, cut precisely just below her shoulders, with a neat blunt fringe falling to cover her forehead. She wore black-rimmed glasses on her high, chiselled cheekbones that caused her dramatic midnight-blue eyes to pop out. They stared out through her thick, bristly black lashes that were slightly tilted at the ends. They appeared like curtains each time she blinked. She was a tom-boy, fearless, fierce, and confident, with a passion for anything scientific. She had a habit of occupying herself with frivolous things mathematical, puzzles or anything science related. She was a person who would always participate in anything quirky or unusual. Then, one day in the middle of university, she decided to leave and find work at the Science & Space Institute, developing new technologies.

Although she was close friends with James, she did not know about the origins of his brother's or mother's disappearance, or that his mother was an alien. Amber was in the midst of working on new scientific AI inventions with her colleagues from the institute. They were constructing artificial intelligence human robots and tiny molecular objects, better known as *nanosomic machines*. These were minuscule motors too small to see with the human eye, but which had the potential to drive innovations in chemistry, biology, and computing. These subjects were her favourite, and she always had the answers.

James, still contemplating whether he should tell Amber about his family, turned with a deep frown and peered at her intently.

"James, come on, what are you thinking about? Now's your chance!"

He paused, and his fear betrayed him. "How? I mean, how are you going to …?"

"Oh, James, you want to bring your brother back, right? So, I will help you. Be decisive, James!" Amber retorted.

"Amber!" said James, quickly thinking of an alternative solution. "I know a better way of how we can get there!"

"Yes, like I said, the Space Agency is to launch its shuttle on the heath," interrupted Amber.

"No, no," snapped James. "I have a better idea. Why don't you meet me at the old school in one hour and bring your Jet-Pack?"

Amber let out a deep sigh. "Yes. Jet-Packs? Amber frowned. What do you want it for? This is crazy. Okay, I'll see you in an hour."

James quickly placed the receiver back on to the telephone and grabbed his worn, black wool jacket, and then he rushed upstairs into Tom's bedroom, rummaging through his cupboards, throwing out boxes containing his brother's sport shoes, books, and cards. James then found what he was looking for. He carefully pulled back the neatly folded pile of jumpers to lift out an elaborate small pot covered with bedazzling, geometric-shaped jewels. He carefully opened the lid and peered deep inside. He blinked as his eyes adjusted to what he had found. He held an excelsior bottle cautiously. "This is it!" He muttered, glaring deep into the bottle.

The liquid in the bottle held indomitable powers. Holding the bottle, he pursed his lips and carefully tucked it tightly into his pocket and then headed downstairs, galloping for the front door.

The light slowly dimmed, and afternoon soon became dusk. James was on his way to the old school where he and his brother Tom had once discovered the entrance to the planets. However, it had been a very long time, and the school was now derelict. James began to feel unsure. It had been abandoned for years, and he wondered if the boiler room was still in its original place or if it had been destroyed.

Anxious that his access route was still visible, he approached the school building and looked around the corner where he could see Amber waiting patiently against the red brick entrance wall. She was carrying her rucksack, which looked heavy, as it dragged on her shoulders. James set off to join her, seeing she had brought her Jet-Pack.

Crossing the main road and darting between the busy traffic, James approached the school, where Amber stood leaning against the wall. She stood strong and robust. She was wearing her black boots with her black wool coat and a blue patterned silk scarf. She appeared quite stylish.

"Hi, did you bring the Jet-Pack?" asked James anxiously.

"Yes, but I still don't understand why you need it?" she replied, placing the rucksack onto the soft, water-logged ground to ease her shoulder pain. "Never mind, come on, I'll carry it for you," replied James while trying to lift her heavy rucksack.

She gawked at James whilst watching his every move as they precariously walked around the school. Something slithered across the ground at speed. "What was that?" asked an anxious Amber.

"Don't worry, I think it's a rat or mouse or even a wild cat!" laughed James.

"Mmm, that's not funny. Okay, great! So, how are we going to get in? It's closed," she said, worriedly.

"Ah, that's where your Jet-Pack comes in," replied James, smiling and feeling confident while still trying to arrange Amber's rucksack onto his shoulders.

"Well, it's good I brought two, then!" she said, pointing to her two Jet-Packs with a broad smile, as if she had accomplished victory in a chess game.

James stared at Amber as he proceeded to lift the rucksack from the wet, old grass, containing weeds and brown deadwood. He grimaced, raising the bag over his back. He then turned to Amber.

"That's why your rucksack is so heavy!" stated James.

"James, be careful!" Amber said, while noting his actions.

"Are you sure it's just a Jet-Pack in here?" James questioned with a deep sarcastic tone.

"Relax, James. It's the Jet-Packs, like you asked."

"Uh-huh, what do you mean, *packs*?"

Amber smiled confidently. "I brought two. I figured we could have one each! Do you want me to get these two working so we are able to fly over the wall before it gets really dark?" Amber suggested, ordering James to comply.

"Good idea, but not yet. We need to walk a little more around the back so we can get to the boiler room."

"But it's getting dark, James. Are you sure about this?" Amber asked, frowning.

"Don't worry," James answered tentatively, lugging

and adjusting the heavy rucksack as he ambled further into the grounds.

They crept cautiously around the old school building, searching for a way in without the floodlights on. It was difficult to see anything clearly except for the silhouettes of strange, wild trees and smashed hedges that emulated monsters and aliens, caused by the streetlight flickering some distance away.

Amber frowned and became worried. She garbled to James, "I am not so sure we should be doing this."

"Relax, we are going to be okay. I know there is a way in. There's got to be," James replied, as he searched for a gap between the overgrown hedge covering the windows at the back of the school.

The moon was in slumber, and dark clouds sprawled across the sullen sky. It was impossible to see anything in the darkness, and Amber became agitated.

"James!" she shouted, "I haven't got time for this! Do you even know what you are doing or where you are headed?" James appeared to be trying to break into the school. Her eyes were wide open, like a wild raccoon, peering through her dark, black-rimmed glasses. Her cheeks became red, and she grew a wrinkle between her eyebrows. Her lips were tightly compressed. "This is not right James!" she protested, feeling anxious and angry whilst watching his every action.

Amber shook her head in despair. She was angry and gawping at the mangled weeds in front of her. James, however, seemed to ignore what she was moaning at and started pulling back some of the overgrown wild hedge and leaped through the paving slabs and old barbed wire. He wandered through, taking giant steps to avoid the stinging nettles, whilst encouraging Amber to follow him.

"Come on, Amber!" James shouted encouragingly.

"I am right behind you, which is more than what I want to do," she snapped in defiance.

They continued walking, driven by their careless curiosity until they came to a built-up, overgrown place where the centre path appeared to descend into the earth. It was difficult to see anything in the darkness at first, but as they walked, squelching the mud beneath their feet through the gap, they were able to see through a deep, overgrown hedge a small light flickering.

"Amber, I think that could be the door to the boiler room," he said, staring into the light shining brightly.

James pushed the rucksack through the hedge to make way for Amber to follow. They leaped through the gap and precariously trudged on. Their feet crunched the ground, squelching, trampling, and stomping on broken rocks.

They turned to glance back at the main road behind

them, checking to see if anyone was following or watching them, but they saw no one, only a silhouetted shadow, thin and unmoving. The huge, dark shadow loomed slowly across the concrete slabs of the outside wall in the shape of a long, crawling object. What was it, man or beast? They neared the entrance, and the shadow continued to slowly come into view. It was enormous, so much so that it shut out every inch of bright light from the streetlamps into a brown tinted smudge covering the walls.

They became roused and rushed towards a back doorway of the old school, trying to get away from the shadow, which seemed to be following them. The shadow seemed to be taking in shallow breaths and then became still as a statue. After a few minutes, Amber became angry and her curiosity piqued.

"First of all, tell me, James, is there really a boiler room? Secondly, do you know where you are walking to? And thirdly, do you know what you have done to my boots?"

She was annoyed and frightened, trying to understand this feeling, as she was normally fearless and strong, yet, somehow, she found herself trapped in unfamiliar territory. Witnessing her new surroundings, Amber became frightened. She gulped, taking in shallow breaths, her eyes radiating a fierce, uncompromising intelligence.

Glancing at James, she whispered, "Are you really sure you know what you are doing?"

James bit his bottom lip, and his face hardened in concentration as he tried to turn the old, locked door handle, which was jammed. "Yes, trust me, I know what I am doing," he replied reassuringly but without a clue.

After not gaining entry, he goaded Amber to follow him to the other side along a moss-veiled trail towards the school block, which was hidden amongst the floor of overgrown trees with creaking branches, rustling fern, and crackly brown twigs. They walked on further and could feel the twigs snap underfoot as the leaves brushed their heads as they made their way behind the school.

"James, I am not happy about this. Are you sure there is a boiler room here?"

They walked on, hearing and feeling the rustling underfoot.

"What was that?" she yelled.

James dipped his head, but he could see nothing except the shadows of skittering mice scurrying across at great speed, causing the leaves to crack and dance off the ground.

"Argh, no!" he moaned. "MICE!"

"Oh, no, hurry up, that's all I need. Find that

door — and quick!" Amber demanded.

Just when they thought they had finally found the correct entrance to the boiler room, the dark shadow reappeared, shooting out against the old shrubbery, shimmering and slamming onto the jagged ferns, causing the shape of a monster dragon head to appear against the brick wall of the building.

James, ignoring the shadow, fumbled his way through the overgrown foliage until he found an entrance door marked 'Gym.'

"Well? Is this the one?" asked Amber anxiously.

"I don't know. We'll soon find out, though," he replied. James carefully placed the rucksack onto the mud, which was pitted and without a single print.

He pushed the door with all his might, his face all scrunched up as he breathed heavily. Frustrated that nothing was happening, he stretched his hands across the door so as to pull the door off from the frame.

"This is ridiculous!" Amber shouted, having lost all patience.

She hastily grabbed her rucksack, unzipped the front pocket, and, with extreme caution, took out a test tube.

"What is that, and what is that smell?" scuffed James.

"This, my friend, is HCL. It's a colourless, highly pungent solution called hydrochloric acid, hence HCL, in water. Have you not heard of it?"

"Well, no," James answered emphatically.

Amber, smiling confidently to herself, glared at James as she began to explain. "Okay, let me tell you about this. It's a corrosive substance. We use this for industrial uses and for space exploration, but right now it will dissolve and rust that stupid iron lock we are trying to open!" Amber looked over the top of her glasses in determination, trying to organise the test tube with caution.

Holding the test tube precariously at a distance, Amber gawked intently at James.

"Okay, just move back, this is lethal stuff. You get a drop of this on your skin, and it will burn it away," she warned.

James took a few steps back, his eyes alert, snapping branches and stumbling over barbed wire. It was an urban jungle with no wild animals, just mice, bats, and the odd hooting owl. Crackly ferns beneath his feet rustled in a cacophony, while his heart raced like a thousand buffalos on a savannah.

He watched Amber in a deep concentrated frown and could see a wrinkle appear beneath the lower eyelids as she cautiously dropped three droplets onto the door handle, then she placed the lid carefully back onto the test tube and quickly tucked it safely into the rucksack. She appeared in control, with a sharp alertness in her eyes, but was still highly pensive and worried that the liquid would not dissolve the lock.

She turned to James and then snatched some large leaves from the ground to wipe and clean her hands. She rummaged through the bag to pull out some wipes. Holding the wipes to her nose, she tried to block out the foul odour.

"Here, you'll need these," she said, thrusting some of the wipes for James to use.

"Thanks," he replied with a scrunched-up nose, trying to block out the foul stench of the HCL.

They watched in fear, standing away from where the droplets had fallen. The remnants were glistening in a clump of old moss, fizzling away. They stood back, their eyes watching it gradually dissolve and disappear into the ground, burning and shrivelling in minutes. The stench of dead wood and the charred flesh of rodents with other small creatures lingered. What remained visible was a wispy plume of grey smoke wafting into the space around.

James sneered, "Amber, why did you bring this? It's lethal."

Peering intently, she replied hesitatingly, "I know it's dangerous. Let's just hope it works." In a few moments, Amber snapped sternly, "Yes!"

The lock started to creak and rust, slowly turning a

burnt orange, then dark brown. It was melting away, layer by layer, crick, creak, crock, the door peeled in slow motion, dissolving like powder. Inch by inch, it began to disappear, leaving a trail of thin, grey smoke hovering, almost as if a magic potion had been released. The stench of raw chemicals, burnt tyres, and old paint stifled the air as it became stronger. They both looked at each other whilst tightly holding their wipes to their noses as their eyes became heavily waterlogged, red, and puffy. Amber coughed away the smell from the chemical, taking a few steps back. James watched in eerie silence as his eyes locked on like magnets as the door began to fall in slow motion. The stench of the chemical was intense. He began to cough and scrunch up his nose, taking in short deep breaths and gasping for fresh air. It was so terrible that even the night light began to tremble.

He glanced at his confident, fearless friend, amazed at her tenacity. There was alertness in her eyes, hidden behind the glasses that sat crookedly on her nose, as she held the wipes against her face. Her eyes became red, stinging and streaming with tears.

Finally, the door burnt away, collapsing and crumbling onto the floor amongst the pile of dirt between the wood panels, twisted bits of metal, bricks, and iron chippings along with rusted parts, all mangled together in a cloud of grey, pungent smoke wafting before them.

The dark shadow could not be seen, but Amber, in her wisdom, turned without hesitation for a split second. Turning around, her eyes burning, she sensed someone or something was lurking. She glared intently through the old Jurassic ferns and the leafy, mouldy canopies, which seemed to guide their path to where they were now situated. Staring sightlessly into the darkness, she could see that there was nothing in front. James began to cough and almost choked from the HCL gasses. She grimaced and frowned, and then they both turned back to face where the door once stood, only now they were in view of a void and charred burnt door, which had fallen to the ground. Their eyes blinked in unison. It was almost as if their journey had now commenced.

"Come this way, and be careful," James said cautiously, intimidated by the dark, splendiferous rock formation towering in front of him.

CHAPTER 11

A Hidden Ingress

James stretched his arm along the side of the damp, mottled wall, trying to find a switch to turn on the lights to the entrance. However, as much as he tried to locate anything in the darkness, he was unable to find the light switch. "I don't think there are any lights, and even if there are, I can't seem to find them, Amber. We are going to have to walk through. Are you ready?"

Amber gave a frowning, worried look, but still followed James, stepping over the old wood planks and burnt rubble. In trepidation, they wandered slowly into the deep cavern.

"It's too dark. I can't see where we are walking," Amber moaned.

After a while of stamping in the dark and frustrated

with walking sightlessly, Amber turned to James. "You must think I am really unprepared," she moaned while sneering. She looked at James condescendingly.

"Here, take this," she said, thrusting her mobile phone towards him. James switched on the phone so that the full light mode shone through into the empty void. A corridor instantly lit up, and large metal pipes floated along the old, broken-tiled, white polystyrene ceiling. Everything seemed a little clearer, though the room now appeared like a ghost tunnel encompassing angled monsters with dragon heads, which were just pipes and objects.

"James, it really stinks in here, and it's a bit eerie," Amber moaned.

"Well, it has been unused for ages. What did you expect? Come on," James said, encouragingly, leading the way through the dark space.

The silence was disturbing, and as the stillness fell over the space, it brought with it a low crackle of thunder with an unnerving nothingness around. There was a peculiar mixture of organic growth and human industry of must, paint, and wood mixed with the scent of vermin, all damp and lingering. It was too much to bear and Amber began to heave. James continued to hold the phone light towards the ceiling so that he could see the wide metallic pipes seeming to dance above the space. Yet his eyes followed the pipes like a pied piper, which, he thought, would lead him to the boiler room, if it still existed.

James continued to pivot the phone into the air. He shone the light into his surroundings out of curiosity. The light from the phone bounced into abstract shapes. Silhouetting the gloomy, dark, deep, space around them. James glared in horror, not knowing who or what he would encounter.

"Well, where is the entrance then?" Amber barked impatiently.

"Follow me, Amber, this way." James led on through the building, searching for the entrance, but with doubt etched upon his face.

They walked painstakingly through the labyrinth of antique wiring and plumbing that resembled a cathedral of horrors. They were blatantly lost, walking nowhere and seeking somewhere. The area was full to the brim with broken wires, which looked like spaghetti, all dangling and draping from every crevice through each laborious step they took. The heavy, thick black pipes coiling around on the ground emulated wild anacondas draping through old cobwebs chasing ants, mice, and anything else that would move. James tried to recall where the entrance was, but in his desperation, it was becoming difficult to locate the exact

Amber leads towards the hidden ingress.

place. He became more and more frustrated. Frowning, he checked to see how much battery power was left on Amber's mobile phone.

Amber turned and gave a cold gaze towards an anxious James. "Well!" she barked again, irritated with his lack of progress.

"Well, we don't have much power left on your phone — that's for sure," James said, whilst holding her phone.

"Well, how much?"

"Twenty-five percent."

"Oh no! Don't you have any idea about this door?" Amber asked sceptically, losing all glimmer of hope in James's actions.

James stared at Amber with a weary resignation and reluctantly admitted, "I can't remember, Amber."

"Oh, for goodness sake, you brought me here with my heavy bag, and now *you can't remember*!" She shouted angrily.

Unexpectedly, her voice reverberated around the dark, broken room. There was a sudden rumble, and debris began to loosen and rupture, falling slowly in front of them, then the falling debris picked up momentum. The whoosh of falling plaster and pipes was like a roller-coaster at the funfair. It blistered through the air en route to its target, and finally, with a deafening explosion, crashed with a boom into the corner of the dilapidated room where they were standing.

"Look out!" James shouted, pulling Amber to safety as the ceiling caved in. There were chunks of plasterboard and pipes falling everywhere.

"Argh, what's happening?" Amber yelled.

She looked terrified, her eyes fixated with dilated pupils, wide open like an owl. She was shocked and began to sob silently, so as not to show her emotion.

After a few minutes, which felt like an hour, everything stopped moving. There was a plume of white ash covering everything, including James and Amber. Their bodies and jackets were totally swallowed in white ash, and they looked like snowmen. However, there was a stillness in the air, an eerie, piercing silence that suffocated where they stood. A cold, damp sense of emptiness ensued, where all that could be smelt was human breath and their human bodies with the faint metallic odour of blood mixed with the remnants of HCL.

James had a flashback, a short, important flashback. He stared, obsessed at the small crack created right in the dark corner where the ceiling had thrown debris onto the wall. They stood like statues, glaring all around them. They were frozen in fear. This was it. He knew it. He blinked a couple of times until his eyes lit up like electric sparks. A small fissure had formed, and hope had returned.

"Look, look, Amber! This is it! I think this is it. I know it is!" James exclaimed while glaring at the small fissure. He strongly felt this was the entrance he had been searching for. His heart was racing, pounding in his anticipation, as his face beamed a red ball of luminosity.

They both stared at the small fissure, their eyes locked in unison for a few moments, turning to face each other in disbelief. Their eyes were wide open in fear, not knowing of the next step that would follow. Carefully, James stepped forward to enter the small cavern.

Amber, watched attentively, blurting out, still in disbelief and pointing to the small gap, "James, there is no way you are going to get through that teeny, tiny space!"

James, listening intently, gawked at her for a quick moment. "Amber, give me a moment, I will show you."

She shrugged her shoulders. It was not long when the same dark shadow they had seen outside the building resembling a dragon's head, or so they assumed, loomed over the covering of the fissure from inside.

"What was that?" moaned Amber. "How has that shadow reappeared from inside the gap? Oh, I don't like this at all. And how much phone light is left?" Amber queried anxiously.

"Amber! Your phone light is finished. I don't know

how that shadow appeared from inside. I am just as—"
James was unable to complete his sentence. At that very
moment, a door slamming was heard, and they both
gasped in horror.

"Now what?" Amber whined.

"We have to get inside somehow," James said, precariously.

They walked on past the fissure. Nervously, James,
still carrying Amber's heavy bag, took deep breaths,
whilst Amber looked on around in anticipation, not
knowing where or what they were walking into. She
opened her eyes wide, trying to focus into the empty,
dull space before them.

"You were right, there is nothing but darkness in
here," she said, resigning to a melancholy tone, hum-
bled by what she saw and amazed at the sense of excitement. James had just finished speaking when a ghostly
purple light fizzed suddenly through the walls and gaps.

Amber grimaced and shuffled across the floor, carefully in sightless sight, still nervous about the mice and
the other creatures crawling along the floor, with the
looming light sneaking through the gaps. Her mind was
riddled in concentration of the unknown.

Unexpectedly, a sharp light was seen streaming
through the crevice along the broken wall. They visual-
ized a protective ball of light that appeared to protect

them against the negative vibrations that they both sensed.

"Quick, stand back, hold on. It's going to really shudder now," James informed Amber, as the whole room began to shake, slowly at first, then it began to speed up, picking up momentum at a high velocity. "Hold on!"

"Hold on to what?" she yelled, all the while looking around her.

"Oh, no, it's a Cosmic Swirl!" James said, rationalising the swaying motion whilst trying to calm Amber.

James held on to a fragile doorframe nearby as everything spiralled and swirled and began to move, revolving at great speed, then it shuddered in short intervals. The room began to move around and around until it all moved like an out-of-control carousel at a funfair.

"What's happening? This is not in any form *rational movement*. Argh!" Amber shrieked furiously, completely dazed and dizzy.

"Just hold on!" James said, shouting his frustration as they both whirled in momentum.

"To what? Argh!" she roared. Amber held out her thin arm, her hand spread out like a spider's limb, trying in desperation to search for a doorframe or anything to take hold of.

James gripped her arm and then strapped his arms

quickly around her svelte waist, holding her tightly. He pulled her towards him whilst trying to protect her from the falling debris. Their faces were soaked in sweat with their eyes locked in a shared understanding. They had become hot, and their faces had turned red from the rush of blood flowing through every vein. Their hearts galloped and raced like wild beasts as they frantically tried to hold onto something, anything, in their search for the entrance to the worlds that James had left behind. The cacophony of falling building refuse and debris was everywhere, with electrical wires dancing and dangling, with short, sharp flashes of light emerging from electrical surges occurring randomly. It was like a light show celebration on a New Year's Day.

They both waited for the spinning to stop, and sure enough, after what felt like a lifetime, it abruptly came to a sudden halt, with everything around them crashing and falling to the ground with a heavy thud. Amber glared, tipping her head slightly to look at James, who still had his arms wrapped around her waist. She took in a deep gulp of air, bravely turning to him.

"Er, you can let go now," she said in a formal, strong, controlled tone, inferring to James, still clutching her tightly, that she was disgusted as to why he continued to hold her.

He smiled hesitantly. "You mean you don't want me

to hold you *now*?" After a short pause, he resigned to Amber's cold exterior and slowly and purposely began to release her from his grip.

"No!" she snapped.

"Relax, Amber, I am only trying to help you — and be careful," he said, watching her cautiously pivot away from him further.

She simply returned a cold stare, trying to correct her pose whilst balancing on the fallen, old wooden splinters with broken shards of glass beneath her boots. She cautiously began to straighten herself up, mindful of where she stood.

There was a deathly nervous silence, and James collected the heavy rucksack from the ground. He goaded a reluctant Amber to follow him. "Look," James bellowed, pointing to the fissure in the wall, which was now much larger and wider than before. It had broken to create a large entrance, almost begging James to walk through. The darkness, together with the eerie silence, acted like two ubiquitous observers, carefully watching their steps.

Amber rolled her mouth, twisting it into the corner. "I can't see anything," she said cautiously.

"You will, Amber, you will!" he said reassuringly. James became euphoric as his heart began to race fast and furiously. He moved closer to the dark hole in the wall to get a closer look. He could only see a dark void. Amber became less agitated, sensing there was something to be discovered through the void in the wall, but James was not moving fast enough for Amber.

"Well, anything? Do you see anything?" she questioned eagerly. James continued pivoting near the entrance to take a good look inside the hole before he decided they should clamber inside.

They nervously stepped inside through the gaping hole so as not to hurt themselves from the splinters in the gap. They took one step at a time over the cobwebs, broken debris, and plaster. Their faces resembled those of lost children. Once they were finally inside the void, they found they sagged into themselves as they passed by the fallen bricks that went on out into a muddy area. Their faces were blank, expressionless, as they trekked through an empty, murky chamber. With old, rusty water pipes and thick wires draping everywhere, it was like an urban jungle of metallic and plastic creepers. Cold silver-coloured water drops fell one by one, echoing as they bounced on the metal. The pipes were hanging like vines only to be accompanied by a dull blackness, and a thick mist silently creeped alongside, enveloping their every move. The sound of silence and the water droplets echoed their footsteps as they crept on through the void, squelching the rotten ground below their feet. They were like omnipresent observers, carefully watching their every move. They didn't know where they were heading. In fact, they didn't even know if they wanted to reach a particular destination, or even if they were heading in the right direction. However, somehow, whether by instinct or intuition, James felt he was closer to Tom, his younger brother. Something was enticing him to walk further, and without much hesitation, he did so. He held his eyes wide open in anticipation, goading Amber to continue to follow him. After walking for a while, they spotted a beam of white light shimmering in the distance. They got closer, the light flickered intermittently, then it disappeared. James gazed in desperation. Perhaps he would not see the light again. Then suddenly, the light reappeared in a bright flash and started to form a shape. Amber peered intently, and then after a few minutes her eyes lit up. She knew what it was.

"That's it. That was the dragon. The shape we saw earlier. It's that dark shadow! James, I know it was!" Amber said, apprehensively. They continued to walk slowly. The shadow loomed larger, and the bright light continued to flicker.

"James, look. Oh, no, do you think it's a ghost? Do you believe in aliens?" Amber asked James, trying to rationalise her anxiety.

"What are you talking about? That is *not* an alien!" James retorted sharply.

James sensed they were near something, but his mouth just locked, frozen in fear of what he was about to encounter. The crevice seemed to hold the secret of his search, or so he thought.

"James, we must be deep inside this crevice, and there doesn't seem to be anything," Amber said.

James turned to her with his piercing, blue eyes, staring intently, hoping she would not give up or indeed stop to discourage him in his quest.

"Come on, please! What's wrong with you? Amber, please! I know—".

At that moment, the infinite space filled with a bright, iridescent light so blinding Amber was forced to quickly cover her face, squeezing her eyes tightly behind her glasses whilst trying to protect them from the sharp, illuminating light. "Argh! James!"

James, half expecting something to happen, gawped at the luminous light with squinted eyes, his face frowning, unsure of the energy source. But sudden and unexpected ripples of fire occurred, burning the floor with a message appearing in lambent flames as it roared across the ground.

"Look!" Amber bellowed, as her eyes almost popped out of her glasses. "There is a message! What does it say?" she questioned with a lingering look to James.

James carefully stepped around the message: *Near is the Fear.* He became pensive. He glared at the message, trying to analyse each word and its interpretation. He appeared strong and resilient, gawking straight in front to a nothingness and then turned quickly back at Amber. The light and the shadow had disappeared, and everything resumed into a solemn darkness. James grabbed hold of Amber's hand. He looked at her. "We are on the right path," he said, reassuringly.

They continued to walk through the dark chamber, pacing slowly at first, trying to contemplate what would happen if something did go wrong or they did end up on the planets and were killed. He shuddered to think about it. Inside the chamber they had discovered it was dark and empty, apart from the fallen debris and mice scurrying around and something dripping in the corner. They both continued to walk through the crevice. They had been walking for some time when James stopped to rest his legs. His face had fallen, and his eyes squeezed together in desperation. Both were tiring, and Amber became sluggish, too. She looked up at the narrow corridor covered in rotting debris and falling pipes and dangling wires. Her high cheekbones were sunken, and her black-rimmed glasses had all steamed up. Her eyes were wide and bright with an alertness about them.

"James, look, look over there!" She pointed to a dark shadow illuminating the wall.

James gawked and his eyes peered around in the shadow until he got closer. He followed the shadow's trail until he saw a mass of thick scales, sharp and bright as glistening ice-like candles, flickering in a cascade of light that covered the ground.

After staring at the shadow for a while, he realized that there was someone or something that was going to lead him to the planets. He became excited and anxious. His blood rushed, and he gained an energy level of a thousand lions roaring into battle. Lost in his anguish, he hurriedly ran towards the light source and what he hoped would lead him to the planets.

"Amber, come on, we are going to have to follow this light!" Suddenly, as their focus was now clear, they both rushed in trepidation, with an energy they thought they had lost. They eagerly marched through the old building, searching for the beginning of the light, when an echo was heard, and the enlightening light shone as bright and fierce as a lambent firework flame. James held up his arms to protect his eyes from the bright light illuminating the space around, whilst Amber squeezed her eyes as tight as she could.

Then it spoke, echoing in a sharp, raspy voice, "James, you already know the truth. The belonging you seek is not behind you, it is ahead. Feel it, sense it in the blinding light. It will guide you. You have always known, be there, and it will lead you to the truth." Then the voice faded away, leaving behind an eerie trail of space.

They stood still, frozen in awe of the bright, white, mesmerising light and the shadowy, gloomy shapes scraping the walls only to fall onto the muddy ground. The old trees spiked at various angles in the dark, like that of a monster or beast, perhaps even a dragon. Amber tried to rationalise the voice she heard, thinking if they were to shake their heads, perhaps it would disappear. She began to think James was hallucinating. She turned to him, but he was fixated with the dragon-shaped shadow.

He shouted out in desperation, "Iktomi, is that you?" There was no response but for an empty silence. Then he hesitated, becoming despondent. "It was him, I know it." He turned to Amber. She closed her mouth tightly and sucked in some air, wanting to talk to James about the shadow, or so she thought.

Amber pursed her lips and frowned, not knowing who Iktomi was. She also did not know who and what exactly she was following, or, indeed, who was following them.

She watched James, clutching at his thoughts so

hard, his face became taut and his eyes pensive and puzzled, forcing his brow to furrow. The shadow had disappeared. "Come on, let's start walking."

As they continued walking through a pitted path, Amber stumbled over a rock.

"Argh!" she screamed. "James, this is a dark place, and to me it looks like a place where no one should enter."

James turned to her. "Yes, it is, Amber! It is!" He stood there for a while, staring at the ground. Then, as if he had just made up his mind on something, he entered the vast void, goading Amber again to follow.

"Amber, I think we will be entering the alien worlds soon," he said.

"Oh, where does it stop?" she said sarcastically, angrily pulling a face. They continued walking, with each step sinking into the waterlogged soil. James peered down at the ground and could not see any mice or animals and sensed something was not right. He turned to Amber, who looked worried. She frowned, pivoting her glasses on the edge of her nose. James grimaced, still holding the rucksack over his shoulder. He adjusted the straps to make it more secure so that it would not move, hoping Amber would be pleased. He gawped at the ground and could see gaps appearing in the soaked, pitted ground. After a few moments, they heard a sudden, loud noise creaking in the walls around them, and with bated breath, they turned to each other, their eyes open wide. The ground began to rumble slowly, then gathered momentum, throwing rocks of differing sizes to tumble and fall. Just as abruptly, several sections of the ground started to crumble beneath them, opening up like trapdoors. They fell, crashing into a rocky shaft, tumbling like a pack of cards, spiralling down into a jagged, dark abyss. They were falling quickly, deeper and deeper, without any warning, twisting and revolving, banging their bodies against the rocky chute, almost like a mash of clothes twisting in a washing machine. They were zooming through the labyrinth, and down they fell, deep into the hidden abyss, screaming in agony.

James, still carrying the heavy rucksack, which he had attached to his back, found the rucksack slamming against him several times as he twisted and rolled through the shaft, whirling and swirling in a kaleidoscope of mesmerising wild colours.

They landed abruptly at the bottom of the shaft. The turbulent movement stopped. They were alive but unhurt. James could see that his black shirt had torn, and his jacket was marked by the rough rocks. He gazed at Amber, who had fallen awkwardly onto the ground. "Are you okay?" he questioned.

There was a pause. "I don't know. I still have a pulse, so I guess I must be!" Amber replied with weary resignation, trying to adjust her scarf and coat.

She straightened her hair and glasses, which had fallen out of shape, and brushed away the cobwebs and dust from her clothing. Her black coat and trousers were marked with scuffs and slight tears. She pulled off her glasses, huffing and puffing in annoyance, trying to correct the frame. Her temperament became roused, and she became very angry. There was an alertness in her eyes, behind the spectacles that now sat crookedly on her nose. After much inspection, she let out a heavy sigh, filled with rage after peering at her clothing. "Oh, no! They're broken! And my boots—argh!" she said, yelling at James.

They both looked horrified, standing in a cold, damp void. There was a deathly, eerie silence that could only be described as an underworld chamber. Amber glared all around her. Her face crumpled, and she began to sob quietly.

"Amber, don't cry," James consoled.

"I am not crying! Why would I cry? I am having a party! My clothes are torn, my glasses have nearly broken! Now get me out of here!" she shouted in a sarcastic, angry tone while grimacing heavily. Her tears started again without sound or movement.

James realised there was nothing he could do for her, so he peered for a few seconds, pulling out his squashed and creased-up tissue in his pocket from his torn jeans. He handed her the tissue sheepishly. He gawked at the surroundings, then glanced down to the floor. He began to see lumps of mottled, muddy sand move quickly, darting one side to another. He nudged Amber to look down at the stridulating movement carefully.

"I want you to get me out of here, and you want me to look at the ground?" she argued, scrutinising the ground. She saw moving splodges of dirt shoot across. Amber had a sudden, eureka moment, a flash thought, a breakthrough. She gestured to James that she was going to disperse a few drops of HCL onto the ground where the movement occurred.

He nodded in agreement, unloading the small container from the bag and handing it to her.

Amber, still gazing and watching random pockets of the ground move indiscriminately, snatched the bottle from James. She began to measure out the droplets of the acid to drip onto the ground.

The moment had arrived, and Amber concentrating, held the droplet steadily over the target she had carefully measured. They both stood still, watching the action of stridulation occur, as if a mole were burying and skittering through. Amber was now ready to release each drop onto its target. There it was. A sudden excitement rushed through Amber as she dropped the acid onto the ground. *Boom! Splosh! Splat!* There was a sudden, loud, dull noise of fireworks. A wild constellation of stars and bright light flashes with sparks zoomed past. The ground began to open and shudder, separating and then suddenly collapsing into a swirling whirl, forming a kaleidoscope of rainbow-wild colours. James glared all around and was dazed at what he saw. He was waiting in anxiety, suppressing his fear. He stared straight at Amber with his blue, piercing eyes wide open like an ocean fixated on a torrent to occur. His face hardened in concentration as he tried to understand what was happening. He watched Amber and how she glared as if an evolving creature were emerging.

"What's happening, James?" she screamed, screwing up her nose in disgust.

"We will be entering, Amber, a deep vortex. This is where extremely malevolent monsters, creatures, and beings will appear from within the dark world. The voice did say to us, *'Near is the Fear.'* They bear no mercy, only malice. There is much evil," James said.

Amber grimaced. She was amazed and wanted to stop and take a sample for her laboratory on Earth, but James insisted they continue walking on.

✤ ✤ ✤

CHAPTER III

THE ENTRANCE

There was a rumble, and with a ferocious roar, the constellation of stars stopped rotating. The zooming stars had passed each nebula floating within the Milky Way. It was followed by a thunderbolt, a sudden flash, and a long, silver, lightning strike. The strike hit the ground with a ferocious boom. It released a constellation of malevolent, mangled shapes of fierce flames in a kaleidoscope of iridescent colours. A loud voice growled again, with an order echoing through the barren land where they both now stood. A deep, raspy voice reverberated all around.

"Such is the nature of all evil. It festers in a sleepless malice in the dead of night. You, James, will return to Moradiya to reclaim your land. Your realm awaits you.

You will face the same evil, but you will succeed, and you will greet your throne!"

James opened his eyes wider, glaring all around him. He quickly turned around, hoping he would see someone, anyone, but he saw no one. The voice echoed before fading away. Amber looked on as her mouth dropped wide open in shock, whilst her eyes frowned in anxiety. James turned to the ground, noticing there was no rubble, no debris, and no wires dangling above. He tipped his head back further into the air to see above him. An apprehension hung like a dark impenetrable cloud as his piercing eyes opened wide in horror. Amber followed in complete disbelief, trying to understand her new environment. He could only see the solemn sky and deep darkness. They were now in view of an empty sky and a dry barren wasteland in front, with scorched rust rocks on a pitted, dry, dust ground, with ridges formed into its surface. It had been clearly marked by old volcanoes, leaving behind the impact of craters.

James knew they were no longer simply walking through an old building. Something had happened. He knew it!

"Look, Amber, look at the ground, look all around you. I think … I think we have fallen into the planets. Which one? I don't know — yet!" he exclaimed excitedly, indicating that the ground had changed. Amber turned her head slowly, glaring at her new surroundings, trying to reason. She stared straight at the large stones formed on the plain. She looked puzzled and confused, but James did not. He had an understanding of what had occurred.

"So, whose voice echoed around the labyrinth?" Amber questioned eagerly, whilst trying to straighten her coat and scarf. James pursed his lips and shook his head, quickly comprehending that the fall through the labyrinth had transported them into the planets and worlds beyond. He soon realised that the voice had beckoned him to the planets. They were no longer on planet Earth, he could feel it. He realised his search and his next adventure had commenced.

A palatable silence passed. The only thing that they could hear was the sound of their own breaths. James took a cautious step in trepidation towards the direction where they had first entered. He felt his muscles at the back of his neck tighten. He took his hands and cupped his neck, trying to ease the lingering tension.

Turning to Amber, he could see her worry lines begin to frame her mouth. They tugged at her eyes through her broken glasses. Her muscles in her jaw bunched together, giving prominence to her high cheekbones. She became pensive and apprehensive at the unfolding events before her.

"You okay?" James asked.

She quickly turned to him, releasing a deep sigh, replying, "Of course. I'll be fine. I am always fine — you should know that!" All the while she was trying to convince her friend of her stable tenacity.

They could see movement in the sky, which looked like black clouds sprawled across the sky, billowing in a wafting, old, dust storm in the colour of a green glow of molecular oxygen. The air grew heavy while the dense humidity pressed down, beginning to suffocate them. Their perspiration trickled down their faces, and they began to loosen their clothing, inhaling as much oxygen as possible. The scent of air felt dark, dank, and intoxicating as stillness fell over where they stood. The eerie darkness of that night would never cease. James clearly remembered the pitch-black curtain draped over the sky, and the twisted, warped shapes that the stars made against the infinite blackness. The milky speckles twirled and danced along the sky in various patterns, tugging at the corners of his lips in a way that almost made him smile. Then a low crackle of thunder was heard. They peered at each other apprehensively as they trudged on. They were feeling sluggish, trying to lift each heavy foot, as the gravitational pull had taken force with each step. They tried to run, but they could not. They were restricted. Something was pulling them back, but was it a gravitational pull or an electrical force? Even though the dusty terrain seemed to swallow their feet, they trudged on. It was becoming difficult, as if they were falling into dry quicksand. They became more and more conscious of the new ground below their feet, making them slow to reach their hideout behind a bolster they were in view of. Amber quizzed her surroundings, instantly knowing that they were no longer on Earth. They couldn't be. How could they be? Earth never had such burnished, brown, dry, powdery ground with jagged rocks strewn across the thin dust together with the rising plumes of warm, green, oxygen-pungent air. The wind seemed to create everything from small dust devils, to whispers of snaky smoke vapours, only to disappear above into the black gloomy sky. Suddenly, for a moment, everything stopped, even something that felt like the wind seemed to hold its breath. Then a streak of hot silver suddenly split the dome in two. A precipitation of soft silver dust cascaded throughout the terrain towards them.

"Where are we, James?" Amber asked, incredulously, waiting for an unbelievable confirmation in his reply.

He peered at her intently and at the dark, empty caverns compared to the dense, bright strands of millions of constellations ringing their edges. His thoughts of trying to convince her of their journey into space without taking the shuttle seemed a daunting task. He was feeling and looking like a lost child wanting to convince his teacher of his innocence. He was in anguish, thinking how he would convince Amber, the friend who works in science and technology. She was practically a scientific astronaut! How could he tell her of the planet and where they were? And convince her! As he took a deep breath and turned to her, a flash of light shot across the terrain.

A thick shaft of green and orange luminous, bright light shot across the ground, illuminating the space all around them. This allowed the shadows of Morkann's evil army of monsters to appear in all their malevolent glory, with their hollowed skulls, pitiful and empty eye sockets, and jaws locked wide open, displaying their teeth in all their bony structure. They were each like a corpse within its grave. They were always ready for a kill. Their ruptured, demonic bone structure dripped gushes of liquid emulating that of saliva, but in close observation, it was dried-up, thick, old blood.

James gazed at Amber. He could see how apprehensive she had become. "Amber, we are—". James did not complete his sentence when, at that very moment, as if by magic, a loud, booming roar in the atmosphere occurred, like the thundering sound of Japanese drums bellowing out as a wild dust storm swished its angry wave everywhere, throwing small particles that landed far and wide whilst sticking relentlessly like Styrofoam packing peanuts. James and Amber covered their eyes and ran as fast as they were able to, dragging their feet behind some large, ridged rocks to take shelter.

They gawped intently, crouching behind a boulder with their eyes wide open, with fear etched upon their faces. For once, Amber was quiet, speechless, and totally lost in shock.

They watched nervously at the scary events unfolding before them. They froze in fear, hiding on the ridged rocky terrain and boulders. James had known they had landed in the evil land of Moradiya. This was Morkann's territory. There was a large dust cloud gathering all around their feet, wafting swiftly. Amber and James moved to hide their shadows from the evil Morkannis. These were Morkann's soldiers. The army of gloom. They were the followers of Morkann and the force of darkness and evil. They were just as evil and malicious as Morkann, their Demon Queen Morkann, who they revered, and if they did not, they would be killed! James precariously tried to glide away along the orange sand dune, but the sand gathered to build a soft mound. Subsequently, it created a track where James once stood, hiding from the Morkannis, causing it to peer at the footprint where James was standing and scared for his life!

James gestured in trepidation to Amber, advising her to keep still. Amber, raising her gaze at the strange figure, was now agog and apprehensive at the giant evil Morkannis, whose shadow stood proud and strong, towering above her. He stood still, while she tried in vain to hide. The Morkannis resembled a skeletal, wild Jinn corpse on the rugged ground. His eye sockets were bulging from his bony, ragged skull, only to display piercing azure darts for his eyes with its overbearing, ginormous skeletal structure looming over the tor.

It came in the form of an inner voice that was powerful. James looked all around him, then quickly gazed at Amber, who was huddling behind the rock. Then, quite unexpectedly, a flash like an intense purple light right in front of James appeared. It was blinding, and James quickly held his hands to his eyes to protect them from the bright glare. A sharp bolt of lightning followed in the night sky, dispersing shining, luminous constellations all around. It was a large kaleidoscope firework at display on a fairground of the sky. This was followed by two very precise yet very surprising visions. James startled and felt Morkann was back to gain her uncompleted war against his family. It was the battle he had once left behind, only to begin again. He turned to

Amber and whispered, "Amber, I can sense there is something strange at work here."

She was stunned, and she glared at James, gulping, asking, "James, who is it?"

"There is something that gives rise to the evil. We are not where we should be."

"What do you mean?" asked Amber.

"I was once told, 'always remember, no one can stand against the darkness alone. After the darkness, there will be light, and after the light comes darkness.' This is the rule of Moradiya, the land of evil."

James knew whose land they were in and where they were. The land was Moradiya, and Morkann was the demon queen of the dark land. She was the one with Medusa hair and piercing green eyes, the colour of the tadpoles making ripples in a pond, that green colour that brings shimmers and traps you into the forbidden, dark land of Moradiya. She was malevolent and turned everything into stone with her evil gaze. Morkann was the malicious one who waited for the demise of his family in order for her to reign the planets. Now she was back with a vengeance. She had always tried to throw her wild wrath in abundance, using her vicious goals.

The Jinn locked his gaze at a petrified James, his blue, sharp, orb darts held within the dark, hollow sockets of emulating eyes. He opened his mouth, lunging forward angrily as if to swallow him up. A tremendous roar erupted whilst James peered to a quivering Amber, who, although startled, acknowledged the completely malevolent, osseous being. She glared intently, her eyes now dark pools of fear mixed in a cocktail of deep interest. Her eyes locked wide open behind her glasses. She began to gingerly slide deeper behind a rock in trepidation. Her cold stare fixed on the grotesque creature produced her silence.

The creature was huge and incongruous, with matted hair and huge, twisting horns protruding upward into the dark midnight sky. The contorted figure eclipsed the stars. It stood on its knotted haunches and stooped as its wrinkled face stared at them. It gave off an aura of pure hate and evil expressed in its dull, dark-black eyes.

The Jinn, elevating in a grey, wispy plume of soft smoke, glided over, trying to intimidate the evil beast. He gave a deep, sinister smirk from his gaunt, grey, gigantic, emancipated face. His hollow eyes locked while his jaw dropped open to display a void of emptiness with his skeletal frame charging forward. Then, from nowhere and suddenly, he duplicated his image, while opening his jaw, emitting a loud booming roar. Only for an army of Morkannis appeared in unison. They all looked up, through the green-purple glow, slowly surrounding their evolving presence. They were looming over both James and Amber who were quivering in terror. Their shadows began to form strange obscure shapes on the rugged ground. Morkann's army, the Morkannis, were all frighteningly perfect and wondrously strong. Amber was agog, yet she was overwhelmed with dread. She watched in horror, as their skeletal jaws dropped wide open. The menacing vulgar visage of their bony structure was like a vortex of hell. They were stomping, and smashing the ground with their protruding bony feet, as if to play out a war dance.

The Morkannis, better known as the Jinn, gawped at James. Their hollow dark eyes beaming out two darts of sharp, blue, piercing light as bright as an azure sea. Then it spoke in a deep, echoing laboured voice, "Feast on the flesh, *convivium de carne!*" It bellowed as its voice reverberated all around. Amber cautiously and terrifyingly watched as the Morkannis sought their feast. A group of them collectively began to surge towards a terrified James in unison. However, James tried to escape from the menacing, marching Morkannis. Frozen in horror, he quickly turned around to search for something, anything where he could hide and feel safe. His eyes were wide open with an alertness shrouding any bravery he may have held. The Morkannis were rhythmically marching towards him, causing the rocks to bounce off the ground. They were like concrete towers, tall, strong, and robust. James was completely terrified as he tried to run past the Morkannis.

"Argh! Quick, Amber, hide!" he screamed, as he approached a gorge, precariously pivoting on the ledge, trying to go behind it. As soon as he saw it, he dived behind a rock on the edge of the gorge. James inhaled some short, sharp, deep breaths as the marching Morkannis advanced before him and began chanting, "*Convivium de carne! Convivium de carne! Convivium de carne!*"

The army of Morkannis did not see James dive behind the rock facing the gorge. When Amber saw James cowering, she knew she had to do something.

"What's going on?" she squealed.

"We are in Moradiya, and that army is going to kill us!" James bellowed, trying to get away from the Morkannis.

Amber rushed to open her rucksack. She pulled out the Jet-Packs and strapped one to her shoulders. Once she had secured the Jet-Pack, she fired it up. A purr of the engine roared. It was tumultuous, loud as Jupiter's thunder. Amber then took out the other Jet-Pack as quickly as she could. Having powered the Jet-Pack, she zoomed high up into the celestial dome, past the Morkannis. The power and bright, luminous flames from the jet caused the stars to form a constellation of shapes. She was amazed. As she flew high into the galaxy, she could see the red from atomic oxygen glow and the Plough constellation in star shapes. "Hey, I know those stars. It's the Plough!" she said to herself confidently. Her Jet-Pack roared, whirring out its radiantly coloured flames, firing out of the miniature exhausts. The ferocious, hungry flames boomed out of the Jet-Pack, illuminating the night space sky with a myriad of constellations spewing out stars, all seeming to dance in the celestial sphere. She excitedly hovered away whilst controlling her Jet-Pack from the Morkannis. She soared near to where James was struggling to get away from the Morkannis. Amber threw a Jet-Pack towards him. "Take it, James!" she screamed.

He watched Amber on her Jet-Pack zoom away. The lambent tongues of ferocious flames wildly roared out. He was fixated in horror at the Morkannis moving closer and at the flames flying out of the contraption. He was in a difficult predicament, not knowing what to do. He turned sharply in another direction, only to view the evil Morkannis lunging towards him. James gasped and turned in another direction, searching for a way out. He could hear Amber calling for him to take the Jet-Pack. His eyes dropped, and his mouth tensed up. He became perplexed as to where and how he could escape. James was frightened and confused. He quickly and at great speed took hold of the Jet-Pack thrown to him. His eyes now carried a mixture of shock and horror as he barely contained his anger. The tor was alight with a green, glowing mist slithering around. It was like the sky had broken. There was an eerie sense that he was in the land of evil. He had to quickly leave and go to where he and Amber could be safe. She called out to him with all her might.

"James! It's all powered up! Just strap it on — quickly, James! Look for the green button!" she said, shouting her instruction whilst trying not to lose her nerve. She was horrified and exhausted, but she felt she had to continue. They were both terrified of the army of skeletal, menacing, evil Morkannis marching towards them, chanting their demonic rhetoric, "*Convivium de carne!*" Amber realised the words they were repeating were menacing, and her thoughts froze in horror. The land she was in was of a dark sphere. She would have to escape with James across the galaxy. But where to? She had no idea. Her mind was in turmoil, awash with thoughts of the unknown. However, she knew it would be with the help of their Jet-Packs, and it would have to be somewhere away from the dreaded Morkannis. It was their only way if they were to survive.

✤ ✤ ✤

CHAPTER IV

THE ESCAPE

James grabbed the Jet-Pack and frantically strapped it on. He fumbled with the Jet-Pack straps and wires, not knowing how to operate it or how to even put it on. He glanced all around nervously, still not knowing if the Jet-Pack was on correctly. He continued watching the Morkannis moving closer to him whilst chanting their menacing rhetoric. "*Convivium de carne!* "Feast on the flesh! *Convivium de carne!*" His face hardened in concentration. Having finally strapped his Jet-Pack on and secured it to his shoulders, he searched for the button on the Jet-Pack to navigate him into the celestial, airspace dome. He agitatedly searched all around the pack. Then a eureka moment occurred — he found it! He pressed the start button together with the green button to initiate the turbo charger. He sighed in relief as Amber hovered above him. The jets began to whirr, and the sound was deafening, so loud that the evil chant of the Morkannis could not be heard. The ferocious flames began to zoom out of the exhausts in vibrant colours of blue, yellow, orange, and red.

James glanced around to see if the coast was clear. It was not; he could see the evil Morkannis had regrouped and were trying to lunge forward to snatch at him with their deathly, bony mouths wide open. They tried to take a swipe at him several times, but as they did, James ducked away, steering his Jet-Pack into another direction. He balanced precariously on his Jet-Pack, flying high into the dark, celestial dome. Their hideous, corpse-like, angry, bony mandibles and hollow cheeks opened in unison to display their wide, angular, bone structure of revoltingly dry, rotten mouths. They appeared withered and not finished, draped in dark matter, as if they had been unearthed from hell. They reopened their huge, dark, hollow mouths to omit an eerie, grey mist of death. It was blinding as it covered up their escape route, which Amber and James were going to use. A string of curses unravelled from his tongue like yarn unfurling as the Morkannis creature advanced. Its golden scales shimmered with his hot anger along with its dark, cold eyes sneering at James and Amber. Every step they took rattled their skeletal physique as they lunged forward in a menacing glare. The Morkannis and their murky, pulsating energy flowing out of their stretched, exposed mouths was too eerie. It had become hard to visualise where James and Amber were hovering. Eventually, they zoomed above as high as they were able to get out of view from the menacing Morkannis. It was difficult for them to view their escape route as the grey, evil mist seemed to have swallowed up their route. The Morkannis became angry, displaying their rage with bellowing sounds and tumultuous marching. They omitted another eerie, loud moan, with their flickering, azure, fluorescent orbs dazzling in torment. Again, they missed, trying to snatch at both James and Amber, opening their dark mouths for another presumptuous meal. James winced and contemplated his escape route, gazing all around. He gawked into the celestial skyline. Feeling helpless, he thought he would never find his brother or anyone who could help him. He closed his eyes, perhaps resigning to his fate and that this was his last breath. Suddenly, Amber soared above James at speed, pulling at his Jet-Pack to move him towards her.

"Argh, Amber! Am I glad to see you! Look, they're moving nearer! They are getting closer to us! It's no use," James bellowed in horror, as his eyes squeezed tightly and his anguish seized his crumpled face, as fear etched upon his face. Amber manoeuvred her Jet-Pack around, elevating towards James so that she was in his view. She hovered around him, only for her to switch on his turbo booster-charger, and as she precariously did so, James sighed in relief, but his tension was too much as they tried to escape. Amber was strong and fearless; she did not fear the inevitable. Then the whirring from the Jet-Pack blasted as it began to blaze out more robust, lambent flames as the turbo booster-charger had been switched on. The rescue mission had worked, much to their relief, as James and Amber got away.

The grotesque Morkannis were left angry and searching while salivating for their next meal. Their beady, fluorescent-blue orbs illuminated like stars that never were. They had missed their chance. James, relieved, had got away as he surged higher into the celestial dome with Amber rising high on the Jet-Pack.

"James, we have to land somewhere," Amber said, shouting her instruction while gesturing.

The Morkannis watched and smouldered in anger. Their deep, hollow eyes opened to an unknown world, black and empty like a barren, desolate land. Their blue, electric orbs shot darts of malice. Their statuesque, macabre, dreary, skeletal figures stood waiting for the signal from Morkann, their demon queen, to terminate James and Amber. They were trapped and petrified, struggling to launch their Jet-Packs quickly away from the planet of Moradiya. They both tried to quickly and frantically glide away from their evil clutches when a cocoon of webbing suddenly covered them. Through the thick, white webbing veiling their escape route, Amber screamed, "James, was this supposed to happen?"

The Morkannis began to poke and prod at James and Amber. The demonic Morkannis were sneering whilst stretching their bony limbs through the blanket of thick webbing until they were able to frantically clamber into and around them. James and Amber were terrified, breathing heavily and gasping in horror whilst trying to gaze all around them. They shrieked loudly, screaming to try and scare the evil creatures away. They held onto each other and kicked their limbs, trying in vain to push the Morkannis away, but the creatures continued to try and snatch at them. Once again, the Morkannis began to recite their deathly chant in unison: "Feast on the flesh of the Carbonites, feast on their *flesh, festum est carnem suam.*" They hollered with each word, reverberating in a slow, rhythmic chant.

Amber dipped her eyebrows, frowning in fear. "James, you've got to do something!" she shouted.

He signalled anxiously to Amber to initiate the super booster-charger on the Jet-Pack so as to surge away from the evil creatures who were trying everything to grab onto them through their menacing webbing. He realised the malice was strong and powerful and that their only way to survive was to escape from their realm — and quickly.

Amber peered all around, only to see thick, white webbing suffocating them. It covered their escape path like a blanket of fog. They struggled to use their Jet-Packs, only to be able to see abhorrent Morkannis' shadows forming in obscure shapes, slicing through the mass of white web. They were still chanting their dismal mantra. James and Amber were petrified. They were unable to see anything through the white webbing except the electric-blue orbs that were luminous through the dense, suffocating, white blanket, enticing them to fall into a hypnotic trance.

"Amber, stay close," James bellowed. The Jet-Packs buzzed and whirred as they spat out a kaleidoscope of raging, fluorescent flames.

James sped away, zooming as fast as he could. He had rocketed so far at such speed that he was now in view of the Clump of Tumblewood, the valley he had once visited. They glided into a cosmic sky and could hear the anger of the Morkannis groaning, shouting, and bellowing their roaring rage, echoing all around. The skyline slowly turned a deathly red, which was a clear sign that blood had been spilt across the realm.

"Amber, I think I remember how to go past these deathly mountains of Moradiya," James said, apprehensively.

"Okay, that makes me feel so much better," replied Amber in her usual sarcastic tone.

However, whilst gliding on his Jet-Pack, he was still unsure. James could see Amber wanting answers. He peered to Amber, who was now frowning and looked angry, but James ate his bottom lip and did not stop. He again signalled to her to navigate over to the ridge of a barren slope. Amber gave a nod and surged ahead, with green and orange flames raging out of her Jet-Pack. They both landed on the rough terrain together.

"What happened just back there? And who were those evil creatures? How do you know this place?" she shouted in a single gulp of air as she began to struggle with her breathing. She gasped for her next breath.

"Amber, sorry. This world is, as you can see, not as it should be. It is a different world. This planet, realm — everything — it's all different, the beings, different thoughts, everything is so different," James said convincingly, trying to persuade her to listen to him and to calm down.

"Hm, you can say that again," Amber interjected furiously. "Well, go on, tell me more."

James had managed to land, but the flames in vibrant colours were still zooming out of his Jet-Pack. He frowned, precariously creeping forward onto the ridge whilst holding onto his rucksack tightly.

Amber frowned as James pivoted on the jagged ridge as he walked nervously towards her.

"Switch your Jet-Pack off!" she ordered. "You're just wasting fuel!"

James searched for the green button, and like a lost child, he looked up at Amber, whose sullen face was not what he wanted to see.

"Amber, listen to me, before you have a go!" James said, as Amber focused on what James was about to say.

"You, Amber, are a Carbonite — through and through," James blurted.

"Carbonite, what do you mean?" she queried, screwing up her face, trying to make sense of what James was talking about.

"People always say that the oldest stories ever told are written in the stars. You know that, right?" James peered intently at Amber, who listened closely. He had now begun retelling his story.

"You're sure of this?" asked an eager Amber, her tense eyes burning into James like two daggers, sharp and ridged.

"Beyond any doubt. This power has been stolen from its heirs. Morkann has lost her ability to take physical and mortal form. Yet, she has the evil to destroy all who confront her — and their powers. The powers of the enemy are growing. Morkann's war on this realm is growing. You saw the enemy and how much malice they carry."

Amber paused and gulped, taking in a deep breath, her eyes still radiant and inquisitive. "Yes, but I don't understand much of what you are showing me, let alone how we got here!" Amber moaned, still baffled by the world she found herself in and the creatures she saw. They both stood on the other side of the ridge, staring into the dark, galactic horizon.

James gave a cold stare and locked his eyes before him. He said, "The stars are veiled, Amber. Something is stirring. We have seen such malice, yet no battle has begun yet. We will need to find the Labyrinth of Light, Amber."

Amber grimaced, eating her bottom lip, and did not speak while pondering deeply about their forthcoming journey.

"Look, some things are certain." A breath of melancholy made itself felt like a chill with a sudden gust from some unknown sea. "There is a time to give up, but now is not the time, and the right time will come, I know. Amber, a mighty war will be upon us," James said in trepidation.

"Why? How do you know?" asked Amber.

"Because Morkann's army, the Morkannis, have seen us. And they will not leave us," replied James.

"Us? What do you mean *us*?" Amber queried.

They stood still, locked in deep thought, staring back into the bright, star-studded horizon. They were regaining their strength from the fierce and frightening encounter with the Morkannis.

"From the ashes of fire and the embers of flames it will be woken, so the Labyrinth of Light will shine bright. From the shadows will spring renewed source of righteous power and the blade will be broken. Then the crownless shall be king," James recited to Amber.

Turning to Amber with a pitiful glare, his eyes dipped and his mouth frowned. "I have seen the wells of the moon, the armies of the righteousness battling with winged centaurs, whilst Chiron led, protecting the virtuous. Great powerful leaders like Aspero, powering through the hues of purple, the colour of kings. The leader of all armies, here in the dominion."

"James, you must know that I am your friend, and I don't really understand how I got here, but I am here now — so I will have to help you, right?"

James looked at Amber gratefully.

"Tell me more about this land. These lands, James. I want to know more," queried an inquisitive Amber.

"Amber, the people of these lands live in fear of Morkann — the demon queen." James dipped his head in anguish. His face dropped as the colour from his face disappeared and his Arctic blue eyes began to melt, leaving waterlogged pools of suppressed tears.

"What is it, James? Why are you so upset?" asked Amber, scrunching up her face.

"Nothing!" James retorted sharply. "How can I tell you, Amber?" James paused reluctantly, his blue, piercing eyes transmitting a hypnotic trance.

"Okay, tell me, what is it?" asked Amber.

He let out a deep sigh. "My mum! She was, um." James hesitated, licking his lips and breathing heavily, staring at Amber intently.

"Morkann eliminated her," he blurted. "How can I tell you? Now, she wants to kill me, and she probably has Tom!"

James paused, throwing his hand over his head and onto his forehead, flickering his brown fringe back over the top of his head, only to close his eyes in solemn despair.

Amber watched her friend reluctantly divulging something that had clearly been locked in his thoughts for a very long time. She knew this information was very personal to him. She frowned whilst dipping her eyebrows. Amber began to feel the pain James was holding. She pursed her lips and gazed around her and let out a deep sigh. "James, I am here with you in this land, this planet. Which, there are, by the way, according to Kepler, three thousand and four hundred different planets last discovered," she said, as she tried to break his solemn mood. "It is a strange place, but I am here, James, and I really don't understand how I got here, but I will help you find them. Don't worry."

After a pause, James trudged on alone towards a jagged, sparkling rock positioned at an angle. James looked across the vastness of the dark terrain, feeling all alone, wondering about his brother and the characters he had once met. Yet, none of them were here.

Amber silently watched him, realising he was caught up in turmoil and battling his questions within. James spoke whilst glaring over the rocky, barren, sulphur-infested land. He turned and peered at Amber with a serious expression, his gaze locked in deep concentration.

"There is something strange at work here, Amber. Something evil, with much malice. Something is giving speed and credence to the land of Moradiya and its creatures. Their dark will is set against us! I can feel it,"

James said in a breathy explosion.

Amber listened intently, watching James in despair peer into the Milky Way to a blanket of luminous points in the night sky, consisting of various shapes and constellations of remote, incandescent bodies like the sun, twinkling, zooming, and flickering. She then precariously trudged across the terrain to join him.

"You okay? Come on, let's go and rescue," she said, trying to comfort him.

James still had his gaze locked across the barren tor before he turned to face his friend. "Amber, I am the servant of the realm, Oblivionarna!" he blurted, sighing in relief. His words trailed off, echoing through the terrain.

Amber, who was by now completely bemused and stunned, glared back at James in wonder. Her bright, bold, dark eyes shone like pebbles on a lonely beach. "James, I don't have a map to Oblivionarna," she moaned sarcastically.

She opened her rucksack and pulled out her Jet-Pack. Turning it upside down, it displayed a small compass. James grimaced, trying to comprehend what she was doing.

"It's my navigating tool. I don't know if it will work here, though," she said, gawping at her surroundings. Then she pulled out the vial containing HCL and released a few drops onto the ground. The ground instantly melted away like snow from a fire. The stench was unbearable as the ground fizzled and curdled, burning away the structure of the minerals found on the planet surface. The clear liquid was left floating in a small puddle.

"What are you doing?" quizzed James with a scrunched-up face.

"Watch. I am trying to see what is underneath here: water, liquid, sodium, something, anything," replied an anxious and fidgety Amber.

They both watched the puddle balance in a crystal ball of clear liquid on the rugged ground, then evaporate into a larger pool dispersing into a bigger space. "Look out!" cried Amber.

They jolted back from the expanding chemical puddle. Their eyes shot wide open and agog like startled children. "I don't think you will find anything here. And I don't think we should be disrupting the ground, either," suggested an agitated James.

"Relax. Look at what's happening," Amber said excitedly, pointing to the liquid dispersing. She had an alertness in her dark eyes behind the glasses that now sat crookedly on her nose. She was lost in deep concentration. James gazed, watching the chemical react with the minerals in the ground. He watched the chemical bubble changing colour into a vibrant cascade of red, orange, and fiery blue. It fizzled into a kaleidoscope of hues while expanding and creating a vast, deep crater. The crater opened in a plateau of black, burnt lava. A gargantuan mould appeared as an eerie, green mist encroached the crater, hovering at speed. A soft wailing was heard, and Amber turned very quickly, correcting her glasses to get a good look at her surroundings.

"There are solid minerals down there, James. Look, below the crater. We can use these flints as weapons!" suggested Amber with an ambiguous smile.

"Look!" James yelled. He peered deep into the crater, only to see stars flickering like small cat's eyes across the concave meniscus of a constellation.

Amber, mesmerised with the vastness of the crater, glared across and then back to where they both stood. It was expanding at an alarming rate. There it was, a deathly pale face, appearing as pale as wax floating. A hologram of death floated in the liquid. *It had to be*, James thought. It appeared human, transparent, yet it was drowning. Its eye sockets closed, and its long, auburn hair wafted layer by layer. Who was it? It seemed to be beckoning to be rescued.

"James, what's happening?" Amber queried in anxiety. "Well, who is it?" she asked, her face crumpled in horror.

"We can't just leave it here! In the water, puddle —liquid. What type of liquid is this, anyway?" she quizzed.

"Amber, it's not human; it's a hologram. It is meant for us to be lured into its trap. Stay back!" he warned in trepidation whilst scrutinising all around him and intently at the walls of the chasm. His eyes, open wide and alert, towering corpses lay buried between the jagged spires now formed.

James, fixated with the image, turned around to an anxious Amber.

"This land is evil!" beckoned a raspy voice. The voice seemed to be echoing through the rocks.

James jumped away from the puddle, trying to locate the direction of the voice. He was concerned that the Morkannis had followed them. Menacing thoughts darted through his mind. They both gawked at their lonesome surroundings, now only in view of rugged, old mountains with pointing spires and cave openings like the toothless mouths of dragons floating in a plateau.

Amber asked again if James knew of the floating hologram in the liquid. "No, I don't, Amber. We have to get out of here."

✤ ✤ ✤

CHAPTER V

ENTERING THE DOMAIN

It wasn't long before the deep, raspy, and malicious voice beckoned again in the distance. At the same time, a green, hazy mist evolved into a dimming smoke, smothering all around the tor. James and Amber wiped their eyes through the mist.

"Who enters the domain of the dead?" a voice shuddered.

"It is I, James, Prince of Oblivionarna," replied James.

"We have been waiting for you. It is you who is the chosen one."

The tall, hooded, sinister figure appeared through short, sharp shards of light bursting into the green, hazy mist. Amber glared, staring at the powerful figure thoughtfully. Her heavy eyelids were a fraction too slow to blink. Her irises too stationary, they were peering through her glasses, locked in position. The creature's fierce eyes, of which there were many, were mad with intense, icy hostility and shot out like warning lights. It gawked, locking all of its eyes at both James and Amber.

"You know the power is beyond your realm, James," it said, speaking awkwardly.

"Who are you?" James questioned in trepidation.

"I am Hydra!"

It was the three-headed monster centaur with the ability to regrow a head (or two) if it was severed. The creature was robust, with the stealth of a thousand lions and the agility of a wild cat on the savannah. It was built like a tower with its three, bulging heads and a Herculean torso on a strong, powerful frame. He tipped one of its heads back, straining the thick cords in his neck, quivering and bulging with rage. Hydra had a violent roar of poisonous vapour as it breathed out evil, green mist, which spilled from one of its vast mouths. It was able to destabilize the senses and block them so that it was impossible to move a muscle or to hear anything. Time froze, and only James and Amber's eyes were now cooperating.

"I have allegiance to Aspero, king warrior to the armies of Oblivionarna and Chiron, lead centaur from the armies of the realm," James tried to say in defiance.

Hydra opened one of his gargantuan mouths, emitting an eerie vapour.

Its heads gently swayed before picking up speed until it fell into a mesmerising trance.

James and Amber looked on in utter bewilderment.

It began to breathe out an eerie, silver smouldering of ice, creating a glacier of dense smog. Then it commenced a power dance, and then the war dance began. Hydra started humming and chanting words that both James and Amber were unable to comprehend. "Can you speak Latin?" James questioned, mumbling his words so that he would not be spotted by the creature whilst grimacing at Amber.

Amber replied, "That's not Latin, James."

The other creatures had all woken up, and his army was beginning to stir, stomp, and rage.

They were all stomping their limbs into the mulch whilst fluttering their muscular arms, of which there were many. Hydra shook his heads, jeering with rage, as the dense smog hazed over the ground.

In the war dance, James could feel their anger while contemplating retaliation. As the dance began to stir up emotions, it filled the other creatures with a profound sense of purpose. Both James and Amber sensed their preparation for battle to commence. Though the ceremony had started, James felt they would have to leave quickly before they were killed.

Hydra and his creatures sang and chanted until they were in a hypnotic trance. Suddenly, Hydra stopped and glared at James intently. He lashed out his limb with a menacing stretch towards James and boomed on the ground.

"I am a Carbonite, no one can command me," replied James, blinking profusely and wanting Hydra to just disappear or vanish into the darkness of the mountains.

But the creature yelled in a deep, creepy voice, "Why are you here in the land of the dead? No more will you reign on our land."

"I come in peace," answered James. "We need your allegiance to rescue Queen of Oblivionarna and my brother. We seek guidance from the Labyrinth of Light!"

"Why would you come and ask for my help? We are the banished ones, the dead! We are the tribe that has been abandoned! The dead do not suffer the living to pass," it raged in a voice that could cut glass. Suddenly there was a sudden silence. Amber gazed all around the crater. Its jagged slices of spikes cut out of the rock formation began to shake and shudder.

James glanced all around him and replied bravely,

"And the living do not fear the dead to ask!"

Hydra proceeded through the serrated, spiky rocks created in the cavern. He passed the menacing creatures lurking between the serrated rocks. They were shadows, peering and gawping, reflecting their malevolent images like razor-sharp mirrors. The images of dead, demon creatures imbedded against the rocky walls bowed as Hydra walked past.

"You *will* suffer me! You will *suffer* me!" Hydra roared angrily as he encroached onto the space where James stood, frozen in fear. Its heads wafting in rage. "You are brave!" it bellowed, its voice echoing within the mountainous cavern.

James stood proud and fearless as his eyes opened wide like Pelican lights. He remained still, his heart racing and his grip tensing in his hand so that each vein protruded like wires in a robot. Suddenly, a crackling and a loud thundering was heard. Amber looked up, whilst her mouth opened wide and her eyes stared at Hydra, who was lunging forward in malice. The mountain began to rupture. The vibration filtered through the chasm, and rocks started to move with the sound of cracks from the broken mountain. The rupture had begun slowly, falling rock by rock, then it began to pick up momentum with a tumultuous boom. The loose rocks were covered in a dreamy, red dust as the mountain shimmered and spat out loose, heavy rocks. Soon, an avalanche of boulders fell vibrating, setting off a sparking of short, sharp bursts of sparkling light, igniting a volcano of fury. It was as if nature's anvil had been struck. The shadows of creatures languishing through each rock began to move eerily and free themselves as if they were brought to life.

"Are you afraid?" James asked Amber. "Be afraid, Amber, but it must not be in fear!" James said, trying to reassure her.

"Remember that, Amber. You will be frightened, often, but don't fear them!" Her face collapsed as if it were a pricked balloon. She frowned wearily.

"Don't worry!" James said, reassuringly. "They cannot kill a Carbonite! They will try and intimidate you. And that's it!" Amber looked puzzled but nodded.

"We are of the light, Amber! Morkann's dominance is dark and full of evil. She cannot destroy us. Well, not straightaway!" James said.

"Morkann! Who is she?" Amber quizzed.

"She is the creature of death. She is a demon queen of Moradiya. She seeks only to destroy and rule in malice. Right now, she wants to oust our family, and she wants to see me, I mean everyone, dead!" James bellowed in anguish.

"You're kidding!" Amber said, listening intently in her usual, sarcastic self, yet still unsure of the wrath Morkann possessed.

James glared at Amber. "You must never stare or look at Morkann, or she will turn you into stone!"

Amber shivered and gawked as her mouth dropped open in shock, and she held her Jet-Pack closer.

There was a deathly silence, and both James and Amber stood frozen in fear, facing the transparent monsters lunging towards them.

"Amber, look out!" James shouted.

A transparent monster appeared from the carved rocks. There were many, each like a corpse within its grave.

"The way is shut. It is made by those who are dead, and the dead keep it," Hydra warned. "The way is shut! Now you must be eliminated!" Hydra bellowed in a deep, demonic voice.

"I summon you to fulfil your oath," Hydra raged. Abruptly, his three, ugly heads swayed, jolting forward almost out of its muscular, gargantuan body. Its protruding eyes glared like a menacing, midnight raccoon, restless and robust. The sinews of his thighs were tightly knit, and his ribs appeared like iron. The creature loomed around James in an intimidating manner.

James grabbed the monster's sword from its bejewelled

scabbard. He pulled at the heavy metallic sword, and after a swift struggle, he held the long sword in his hand. It sparkled like a constellation of stars, shooting as if red sparks were spitting out from an anvil.

"Amber, run!" James screamed.

"Run? Where to? Why is it you are always meeting these creatures? And I thought they were the good guys," Amber questioned angrily, as she tried to run away.

Meanwhile, James aimed and plunged the metallic sword into Hydra's transparent, green body.

The three-headed monster let out a booming roar. The demon squealed and cried out, "ARGH!" He let out a roar so loud that it echoed and seemed to bounce off the mountain as a glacial pang of pain, like the stab from a dagger of frozen ice from a poisoned well had been shattered. The creature continued to howl in agony, throwing his arms up in the air in sheer pain. Each head began to fall and lolly around, dropping and flopping from side to side, slamming and crashing with unbridled violence. The heads fell from different angles, slicing the ground with a tumultuous boom. It fell onto the mineral ground as if in agony, breaking the infested rock into a thousand pieces. It was like the shattering and splitting of a mirror. Its voice filled with a dark, intense rage as it echoed through the gorge to beckon an army of deathly, skeletal, translucent creatures. They appeared with half-finished faces, tempered like steel, but with mottled skin. They were many, and they seemed to appear from nowhere, grunting, stomping, raging, with a cacophony of monstrous yells and grunts, some screeching and hissing. Yet, all were hypnotised and seeking revenge. Even so, Amber slid around the rocks in the shadows until she was closer. The figures were feet away, but all she was able to see were transparent holograms of green, misty figures. Even the eyes were still and rock-like, inhuman and half finished. They pounded and trampled the ground as Amber grimaced and gave a sullen stare. She paused as a deep question about the mystery of life overtook her mind. She gave a distinct glare, which was the only message James needed. She hid behind a rock, not really knowing where to go as she watched the deathly creatures step angrily towards James, their mouths open wide and their arms stretched out, ready to pounce on him as they lunged forward with their ferocious fight etched upon their faces. The walls rose, and the noise became louder. The plateau appeared wider, larger, as the sounds grew into a tumultuous cacophony of noise, faster and angrier, with the sound of screeches and unearthly laughter, shrieks of terror, and cackles of mirth, howling and roars surrounded the tor.

"Watch out! They are moving fast, James!"

James stepped back in trepidation towards an exit in the crevice. There he spotted a small, clear, bright, white light flickering like an iridescent soap bubble through a gap. His heart raced as his breathing increased. His mouth dried up like straw. He licked his lips and looked up at the fissure in desperation where the bright, white light still beamed through. He could feel something had arrived that beckoned goodness. But what was it? Maybe it was hope.

Amber turned to face a large group of transparent monsters marching towards them. James took a few cautious steps towards the light, but the moment was not right. He could sense the shrill of fear, and after hearing the empty, droning sounds of the monsters screeching, he could see nothing but blackness, the vast, empty blackness of the awful, looming, night sky. Amber peered intently and was suddenly grabbed by a long, fluorescent-blue feeler, writhing and squirming and pulling at her legs. "Argh, get off!" she yelled, kicking her legs, pushing the feeler away. She eventually slid across the plateau discreetly, hoping to get away as quick as she was able. In their anger, the roar of the monsters echoed through the gap while a blue-tinged light seeped through as each tentacle slapped the plateau in rage. James entered the plateau while a shimmering wall of the black rock from the plateau split into two huge mountainous rocks. The split creaked and roared, shaking the ground whilst releasing a grey, soft, dreamy smoke sluggishly wafting into the surrounding space.

"It's the Labyrinth of Light. It's in the gorge, Amber!" shouted James excitedly. The monsters marched on, throwing their fluorescent-blue tentacles around, but as they tried to catch Amber, they missed her waist, and she was able to slither out of their grasp. The monsters had failed, and they roared with a mighty boom, knowing that their effort was without success.

James watched and listened to their sounds. They snaked forward towards the creatures, or were they the enemy? And as James did so, his skin crept and grew damp. "Are you okay?" questioned James to Amber.

"No!" she bellowed angrily, peering into James with deep contempt.

James could not help but stare at the muted rocks of bodies embedded within the stone. The creatures were sitting on the broken ridge in the dawn, half smoking in their tattered rags, like failed, sectarian suicides. Their icily cold, stretched-out hands were as clammy as death, with their faces as pale as wax. The other creatures would come to help them. It was known that a year ago there were fires on the ridges and deranged chanting. The screams of the murdered were etched upon the rocks and on the deathly creatures. They were fatigued, faded in the lustreless air, as of a caged creature. By day, the dead were impaled on spikes along the rock. The images were of something too abhorrent to see, yet a constant curiosity was pulling James. What did they do? Who were they? He thought that in the history of the worlds he had found, what, was it all because of Morkann and her evil menace? He wondered. It might even be that there was more punishment than crime, but he took small comfort from it.

"Come on, we have to enter the Labyrinth of Light! That light, we have to follow it!" James retorted, pointing to the white light still beaming and beckoning to them through the fissure.

Amber hesitantly trudged through the glacier ground, following James.

"James, who is Iktomi? You mentioned him when we arrived."

"Iktomi! Oh, where do I begin?" James turned to face Amber and stopped moving. It was all coming back to him, almost like a wild bird call.

He paused, taking in a deep breath, and then turned to face his anxious friend.

"Listen, sit here," he said, pulling Amber to the ground to sit on the rock with her rucksack. "Let me start. The story goes, long ago, when the world was young, an old spiritual leader was on a high mountain. It was on that mountain he had a magical vision. In his vision, Iktomi, the great trickster was a crafty chameleon. He was a sage, a teacher of wisdom. In the vision, Iktomi would appear in the form of a slithery spider. Iktomi spoke to him in a sacred language only the spiritual leaders of the tribe would be able to understand. As Iktomi spoke, he took the elder's willow hoop, which was adorned with feathers, horse hair, beads and various offerings. Iktomi then began to spin a web. He spoke to the elder about the cycles of life and how we begin our lives as infants. We then move on to childhood and into adulthood. Finally, we go on to old age, where we must be taken care of as infants, thus, completing the cycle. Iktomi warned, whilst he continued to spin his web." You see, in each time of life there are many forces, some good and some evil. If you listen to the good forces, they will steer you in the right direction. But if you listen to the bad forces, they will hurt you and steer you in the wrong direction." James paused and stared at Amber as she listened with a deep understanding.

"Amber, you must understand the forces of good and evil are so much more apparent," he continued. "There are many forces and different directions that can help or interfere with the harmony of nature and also with the

Great Spirit and all of his wonderful teachings. All the while the spider, the crafty chameleon, Iktomi, would speak." James saw that he held Amber's attention. "He would continue to weave his web, starting from the outside and working towards the centre. When Iktomi had finished speaking, he would give the tribe elder the web and then he would say, 'See this web here. It is a perfect circle,'" said James eagerly, as he continued reciting the story. James stopped telling the story and pulled his heavy rucksack towards him.

"Look at this. This is it!" He pulled out a dream catcher carefully from the corner of his rucksack. He handed it cautiously over to Amber to hold.

"This is it. This is the one I had when I was with my brother the last time I was with him!" He hesitated, breathing deeply. Nets of wrinkles at the corners of his young eyes suddenly appeared, making them water-logged.

Amber held the willow hoop wearily, which James gave to her. Within a moment, she was engrossed with the strange object and was inquisitive to find out so much more to the story as James recited.

"But there is a hole in the centre of the circle, James," Amber said, pointing, after she examined it, turning the hoop upside down inquisitively.

"Yes, I know." James took a deep breath and sucked

in his cheeks to continue. "Yes, it is said that you can use this web to help yourself and your tribe, I mean friends. You know, Iktomi always said that to reach your goals you have to make use of your people's ideas."

"What do you mean?" asked Amber with her voice creeping under her breath.

"Things like dreams and visions. It would be all about the Great Spirit." James gave a nervous smile, chuckling hesitantly. "You know, it is written that as Iktomi was spinning the web, he would say that this web would catch your good ideas, and the bad ones will go through this hole."

He started flicking and playing with the dream catcher and pointing to the hole created through the beads that were connected together, enticing Amber to peer closely.

James became quiet and turned to Amber for perhaps comfort or understanding. He had become increasingly demure. James handed the dream catcher to Amber carefully. He watched her hold it and turn the dream catcher in her delicate hand with care. She continued examining the strange object all the while wanting to say something. Yet, her character did not comply. She was too stubborn. However, she wanted to say something, anything, just to comfort her friend.

"Erm, James, I just wanted to know if you, er, ask if

you, er, umm, were okay?" questioned Amber cautiously.

James was startled in her response and gazed up at her. In many ways, he was relieved she was human!

"Amber, um, it reminds me of when my mum died and my brother was taken. It's just that all those memories coming out are too hard to put away. Sometimes it just gets too much! It feels like I haven't been communicating that with you," James said in a hoarse voice whilst suppressing his melancholy grief.

Oh, I'm sorry, James. I am sorry. I didn't know," replied a sullen, upset Amber.

"No, no, it's okay, you didn't know. Amber, everything is about to change. Everything!"

She looked up at James with her eyes wide open, like a raccoon.

"We are looked upon like some sort of demigods!" James moaned as he retrieved the dream catcher carefully from Amber.

She blankly looked on, wide eyed, her fragile, thin fingers bowing to give the dream catcher back. James stowed it back into the corner of his rucksack as carefully as he took it out. After all, that was the only thing that remained of his brother. A reminder, that he once had a sibling. James had to keep it safe.

Suddenly, a dazzling shower of shooting light

streaked across the space dome above, erupting in a fountain of stars. Rumblings with moving shadows appeared in the space above and all around them. The brightly coloured, shooting star rocks whizzed past from all different directions across the Milky Way towards the red star Nebula. They watched the dazzling, obscure event. Some of the stars vaporised into the atmosphere, and a small part of them fell to Earth as dust. They had wandered deep into the chasm, mesmerized in a hypnotic swirl of stars in flamboyant, iridescent colours. As they peered deep into the cavern, they could see the opening to the fissure. The spellbinding light still protruded through the crevasse, sparkling and brightly illuminating their route and beckoning them to walk on ahead. The sound was loud, like the wrath of war, only this time they could see it, too. The lights rolled into a baleful constellation of stars swiftly moving in vibrant shades to create an aura. James shook his head nervously. He scaled the chasm and realised it was time to leave the desolation.

"Come on, we have to go from here. We must go *now!*" he said abruptly, as he scanned the chasm in front of him. Just then, he caught sight of the strange, deathly creatures moving towards them. It was hard not to notice their mad, staring eyes protruding from their hideous, bony skulls. Amber seized her rucksack in deep anguish and with fear etched upon her face. She stood up quickly, her eyes locked in deep concentration. She was ready to follow James.

"These demon beings will kill us if we don't get away from here quickly!" said James in a calm, unhurried voice.

"So, where are we? And what's happening?" Amber questioned.

"Astral Dimension, Amber! Astral Dimension! That's where we are! It's a place where the soul can exist away from the body."

"You mean, nothingness and absoluteness, the link between heaven and hell?" Amber retorted, giving half a smile and then retracting her words quickly.

James gave a sudden, cold stare. He could detect distress in her voice, and anger, but also curiosity, which was what he had always admired. James realised this was the right time to advise Amber of his sibling and of Morkann and that he was on the right route.

"Moradiya has many deep crevices and gorges. You saw them, right? We will need to pass them before we can get out of here." He looked up anxiously at her.

Amber, not completely satisfied, gave a grimacing stare and rolled her lips.

"I will explain later. Right now, we need to get back to the fissure with the light and out of here, quickly!"

suggested James.

"I hope we don't bump into Morkann. She will appear soon, I know it. She has the ability to take any form. She is an evil shape-shifter, a chameleon. We must just be careful not to look at her eyes!"

"Why?" questioned Amber.

"She will turn us into stone, if she doesn't kill you first!" replied an angst-ridden James.

After much pacing around through the rugged terrain, Amber grew tired of walking, feeling they were meandering in the same direction.

"Oh, James, let's face it, you don't know where you are going, do you? Do you know your way, or not?" she moaned, with a touch of sarcasm in her voice.

"Amber, there is no map, is there?" answered James, who was now flustered and frightened. "Look, I know you may feel this to be odd, but you must believe me when I tell you, I know where I am going and I know where I am."

"I told you I am a prince and … these creatures. I don't know how to … how do I tell you? You are just going to have to trust me," he said, pleading. "Come on, Amber, we have got to go from here," he said, scanning the strange tor all around him.

He seized his rucksack from the ground, enticing Amber to do the same.

She took hold of her rucksack whilst glaring at James, all the while just thinking about his dilemma. As she was about to place it over her shoulder, a rumble and a flash of silver sliced the galactic space above.

"Argh! What was that?" she said, startled and dropping her rucksack.

She stooped to clutch her rucksack and delved deep inside it to pull out the test tube containing the chemical HCL. She took hold of the test tube and carefully held it so that the pipette was able to spill two, small drops onto a jagged glass rock next to where she stood.

James frowned and seemed very puzzled. "What are you doing, Amber? This is not the right time!" he protested angrily. His voice trailed off, but the conclusions were inescapable.

Amber felt she had to do something. Feeling compelled, she continued, "Just watch, James."

Amber took hold of the chemical carefully. She spilt two drops onto the stone. At first, it sporadically smothered the grey, glass stone, shimmering as it covered it in ripples. The clear, chemical liquid slid onto the ground on either side, almost as if it were icing on a cake. Both James and Amber glared in trepidation. They were locked in a trance, watching the chemical liquid smother the rock.

"We haven't got much time, Amber! And I don't

understand," exclaimed James, who could see Hydra's shadow marching in the distance with his army. After a few minutes, the flames appeared slowly, then they began to change into a bright yellow, blue, and orange flare, igniting and burning slowly. It raged violently, spitting out its ferocious blaze. It sparked, only for the fierce fire to reveal intermittent images of dark shapes with wild, unfinished faces mangled together through each flame. They watched, gawping in trepidation, as the fire turned the stone eventually into a clear liquid. Finally, it happened! The raging flame took hold of the stone, disintegrating it into the raw, chemical liquid bubbling onto the ground. It began to form weird shapes until the masks of devilish felons wrapped themselves around the chemical. Then, just when Amber and James thought the flames had ceased roaring, a spark erupted. It changed colours into sapphire and gold, roaring and raging uncontrollably, forming a gargantuan hand. The hand was ambiguously crooked as the liquid was locked into a shape of vengeance. Then it grew and strengthened, becoming longer, stretching and extending into a heavy spear.

A weapon had been created.

Both Amber and James shot back from the stone, watching in apprehension as each event developed.

"What's happening?" asked Amber.

James gazed at her, his face tempered like steel and his eyes locked like rock.

She gawped at him and all around, noticing there was a dangerous stillness about him.

James turned to his friend. "Who knows what you've spoken to the darkness? In bitter watches of the night, when all your life seems to shrink, the walls of your dell close in about you," he bellowed in desperation.

"James, we are going to be fine!"

"It's the spear! That's what's being created, magically!" suggested James excitedly.

"Wow! So, here we have landed in space? I have seen it all now James! You know, it's difficult to see space-time. Because it's curved in a way that humans cannot see," Amber replied.

This was the first sign James had received that there were many hands involved in the death of his mother and the disappearance of his brother.

James grabbed the glass spear from the ground.

Amber, turning quickly, could see a large gorge covered in a purple light emulating an entrance.

"Look, James!" she said, pointing to the gorge in the distance. It was flickering its purple haze.

"Um, I think, Amber, that is the Sacred Mountain. It's the opening to the Secret Alliance of Thirteen Sages! Come on."

They set off in the direction of the gorge with its purple light gleaming through, brighter and brighter. But James was still concerned about Hydra, who was still in pursuit with his deathly demon army.

They trudged on through the rugged terrain. Hydra seemed to be closing in with his army following obediently in unison behind. The clunking of armour and shields with heavy feet pounding and thumping the tor could be heard. James and Amber could hear them and see their poisonous, green haze following behind. They walked closer to the gorge. Amber could see a metal frame shimmering in the distance.

"Wow! Look at that, James. I think it's a Faraday cage! But what is it doing here?" she questioned.

"Well, that's great! But what is it?" asked a very inquisitive and puzzled James, who now was completely baffled by the strange contraption they were now in front of. The fact that Amber did not seem to be worried about the demon beings in close pursuit James found baffling.

"Goodness. Don't you know? I can't believe it!" replied a confident Amber.

"Well! Tell me then, quickly. What is it?" quizzed James.

"It's an enclosure used to block electromagnetic fields, and it operates because an external electrical field causes the electric charges within the cage's conducting material to be distributed," Amber said with a broad grin across her face, her eyes wide open and alert, almost popping out of her glasses. But she was disillusioned. She was unable to understand why the Faraday cage was in space. She began to ask herself how and when. Amber frowned, thinking thoughtfully about her last expedition to space. Her fear was etched upon her face as she turned to James.

"But what's it doing here?" she questioned herself under her breath.

"Look, how is that going to help us?" asked James, staring at the strange, metallic cage.

"The compass, James, it will tell us where we are in space!" Amber retorted. "It cannot block, stabilize, or slow varying magnetic fields, such as the Earth's magnetic field. So, I think my compass will still work. You've got one too, right?" she asked James, her face crumpled in anguish.

"The compass will still work inside. I am sure of it. You know, they are also used to protect people and equipment against actual electric currents, such as lightning strikes. A much-needed resource! You saw what happened." Amber gazed at James, feeling he should be able to recall the light striking earlier. Suddenly, she came alive. She had returned to Amber the scientist who was as agile as a leopard and as bright as a spark.

The dark *Caedes* from the deathly Tower of Belle Noir were languishing in the crevices. They appeared like figures made from rock carvings. Their grim faces were rotten in parts, falling flesh and rotten teeth smiling with severe malice like they were wearing masks of hell. They were all hidden in between the clefts of rugged rocks, lurking and ready to pounce in their menacing manner. The creatures would appear randomly, forming shadows and trying to escape their desolation. James scrutinised all around him, trying to locate a new escape route back to the illuminating Light of the Labyrinth through the fissure.

CHAPTER VI

A Clash of Light

"The armies will soon be here with their wrath! It will be too much to surpass. They are moving at speed and quickly now. We will not be able to stand against the might of the Morkannis, nor these death creatures!" suggested an angst-ridden James.

"James, we could use our Jet-Packs to get out of here. Don't forget, we still have power in them," Amber said, excitedly.

"Yes. No! I mean, I don't, umm, what I mean to say is, I don't think there is enough power left in them," replied an anxious James, trying to recall the last time they had used the Jet-Packs, but he was completely pre-occupied with Hydra, Morkannis, and his personal mission.

"But James, we are going to have to get out of this Pocket Universe!" retorted Amber, as she stared in repulsion at the spiky, grey, evil mountain ahead of their route.

"I know! Let's just move out of this land and continue to the Secret Alliance towards the Sacred Mountain!"

Both James and Amber continued in their steps, turning to check that their route ahead was clear.

But without warning, a bright, scorching light dazzled very near to them. A deathly creature appeared, hovering over them in a menacing glow. James stared up at the eerie, demonic creature and gave a troubled look at Hydra. Amber began to sense the anger in the creature wanting to attack.

Hydra walked over to James, glaring with his steely eyes. "You underestimate the power of the dark side!" he roared in anger. James glanced all around him, watching the creature lure and jeer at Amber and James. Suddenly, he heard a heavy metal clunk and the drawing of a dazzling, heavy sword in the nebula light.

A fearless James gazed at the tall, monstrous centaurs. The centaurs, who had shoulder-length, straggly, black, coarse hair to their broad, robust shoulders, stood proud with their thin waists like a man's, with their strong, six-pack torsos, lean and pounced, but their legs were shaped like that of a goat's (the hair on them was glossy, bristly, and black) and instead of feet, they had hooves, like that of a horse. James listened carefully, not knowing how he would escape through the plateau. The creatures gathered around menacingly. They were incandescent to gaze at, with their bold, black, wide eyes open and alert. James took the spear and aimed it towards the stars, trying to reflect the light, which then bounced back into a sharp prism, reflecting back into the silvery orbs of the demonic creatures.

"Argh!" they screamed, flapping their arms and leaping all around.

"Amber, power up your Jet-Pack, quick!" shouted James.

"But James," yelled Amber with fear and anxiety etched upon her face.

"Just do it! Quickly, before we both get killed!" James ordered.

At great speed, Amber fired up her Jet-Pack, and it roared, rumbled, and whirled, spitting out bursts of white, yellow, and blue iridescent flames until Amber stood on the stand ready to levitate into the air.

The creatures jolted back in amazement as they were overpowered in bewilderment, appearing completely baffled by the contraption. They watched how she commenced to fire up the engine and initially ascend slowly, then to gain speed. James hurried away, dodging between boulders scattered across the terrain. Brandishing his spear, he held tightly into the stars, hoping to reflect and shimmer the light as a prism as much as possible into their orbs as a deterrent. He needed to just deter the creatures enough for him to rush like a cyclone to grab onto the bottom edge of the pack cylinder, where Amber stood waiting for James to snatch onto her pack cylinder. The Jet-Pack swayed with the weight of James. It lost its balance, skimming past the heads of Hydra.

James could see the Jet-Pack hovering above while the creatures tried in vain to seize them, snatching at the pack. James quickly pulled at the corner of the Jet-Pack cylinder to quickly jump on. Holding it tightly, his legs dangled precariously, he got away.

Amber had already opened her rucksack. She frantically and hurriedly connected her Jet-Pack. She tied up her Jet-Pack to her back and began to ascend higher and higher into the celestial air whilst the Hydra remained below, roaring with rage.

"Arrrgh! What are you doing?" Amber shouted in anger, trying to realign her Jet-Pack as she zoomed away.

"Moon rises to its apex as a rare celestial moment of

the planets. That means, Amber, we are approaching the Sacred Mountain. Look!" bellowed James in relief.

Hydra let out a terrifying, ear-splitting roar and lunged towards Amber in anger, stomping the ground and shouting a violent rage. Its heads lolled and fell to the ground. Its malevolent eyes, of which there were many, were all open and fixed like Pelican lights, beaming and flashing with malice.

"All the powers of the galaxy will be invested in me. I will reign, and you will cease to exist! It is my destiny, my right. You will disappear, just like your mother!" Hydra bellowed. Unable to hold back his wrath, he hurled his fist into the air. His army of deathly creatures continued to try and snatch at the cylinders on Amber's back as James dangled from one of them, kicking out at the creatures.

Amber glared gobsmacked towards James. She was in total disarray, trying to comprehend his tragic story unravelling before her. She quickly navigated and manoeuvred as fast as she was able to away from the demon creatures, with James still dangling from her jet cylinder. She decided to locate a quiet space. She hovered over a gorge, and bearing to the right of her, was a large plateau. The creatures were no longer in sight, so she rotated and began to descend.

"Hey, what are you doing?" shouted James, alarmingly.

"James, you can get your own Jet-Pack out now."

"Yes, Amber! I don't think I have enough power in mine, though," James replied as he descended.

"James, open your rucksack and check. You should have about twenty-five percent! A quarter of a tank full. Come on, before we meet any other weird aliens," Amber instructed, stormily.

After landing, James withdrew his rucksack from his shoulder.

"Why did you stop?" he queried with a puzzled look. James slumped onto the ground, dropping his glass spear. He quickly stood up, dusting himself down.

"It should last for another thirty minutes," she said in determination whilst scrunching up her face.

"And don't forget the spear!" she said as James connected his Jet-Pack onto his shoulders.

The Jet-Pack whirled and whizzed, roaring as bright flames bellowed out of the cylinders. He took flight and zoomed into the sky.

James looked up at the empty, dark horizon in front of him, knowing he had little power in his Jet-Pack and little time. He wondered where his brother and mother could be. Grasping his glass spear made from the rock and the chemical HCL, he frowned as he thoughtfully stared at the spear.

Amber, realising James was distraught, approached him.

"James, you once told me you will find your brother. You cannot falter now. Trust your instincts, James — you must!"

James let out a deep sigh and glared at Amber. "Thanks. We must get to the Sacred Mountain. I think it is near. If we do, I know that it will lead us to the Secret Alliance of Thirteen Sages. Come on — you trust me, Amber, don't you?"

Amber hesitantly agreed and followed him like a lost stallion.

They zoomed through the galactic airspace on their Jet-Packs. Solar flares with sudden flashes of brightness rocketed past them, whirling and rotating like a wheel in a firework display. They hesitated and stared into the distance, their eyes locked like flashbulbs following their path.

"What was that? What is going on?" Amber shouted to James, as she watched the flash of light zoom past them in lightning speed.

James scanned the space before him and behind, gazing deep into his memory. The terrain rose up all around him. Jagged, mountainous rocks were standing proud on a tectonic plate like the cathedral spires of an ancient ruin. The rocks were large, with colossal boulders falling into giant monster-shaped figures to form canyons, paralysing the movement of the tectonic plates beneath them.

The light flashed again, and quickly, without whiz-zing and whirling away, it hovered above in the galactic airspace. Pink, yellow, green, orange, and blue irides-cent, bright colours danced like a kaleidoscope from lost stars, rotating in a mesmerising trance. Both Amber and James turned to each other and took off their Jet-Packs. Staring coldly at each other, their eyes open wide in wonder, they contemplated their next encounter.

"What is it, James? What are you looking at?" que-ried Amber.

"Come on, let's go this way," he said, pointing to a bright, white light beaming through a fissure like a bea-con. He ambled through the rugged path towards the solitary light source.

James quickly glanced around to make sure Amber was following behind.

"Amber, what are you doing now?" he said, peering at Amber kneeling on the floor and placing some rocks into a small pocket in her rucksack.

James scowled, "Amber, what are you doing now?"

"Relax, James, I need some specimen dust, so I can analyse them when I get back to Earth," she said while hurriedly topping the small tube with ground dust. Her glasses slipped and pivoted at the end of her nose. She looked up at James and smiled. "Come on, I got it!" she said, as she packed the container with rock dust.

James walked closer and closer until the light beckoned, shimmering and flickering out short, sharp, burning light flashes.

Then he heard a deep voice.

"James, we have been waiting for you," the voice bellowed, as it echoed through the galactic space. Again, the voice reverberated and bounced off the rocks.

"There will be times when you may feel powerless. You may look at some of the demons and danger that is happening around you and feel scared. Just remember, in darkness, all it takes is one flicker of light to create the right path. Don't let fear take root in your heart. Instead, confront it, no matter how frightening it seems. Don't allow hate or fear to win!"

The voice trailed off, and Amber stood still as a statue in shock. Her eyes locked wide open like flashlights gazing through her glasses.

"James, do you know who is saying this?" she asked, incredulously.

"No! Look at that light!" James shouted, mesmerised by the light source beckoning him closer. He ambled cautiously towards the bright light.

"James! James, where are we?" questioned Amber, watching how James had fallen into a hypnotic trance. He seemed locked and possessed with the light.

Ezekiel appears in a green haze of intrigue.

A sharp ray of bright, white light dazzled through the vast darkness of space before James reached the light source.

"Prince James, we welcome you. I am Ezekiel!" The voice spoke in a loud, raspy shrill, whilst holding a ball of wafting, wispy smoke in the palm of his hand. He was wise and old, appearing as a strong noble wizard.

The light dispersed away, only to display a tall, robust, robe-covered creature. Ezekiel emerged through a blue-green haze. He sauntered closer towards James and Amber. Although he towered over James, he was like an emblem of goodness.

His skin was purple. He appeared as strong and robust as an ox, towering over both James and Amber. He was covered heavily with a thick, dark robe. He stood bold and sturdy, holding with his right hand a wooden, rustic staff, at the top of which were two sharp horns and a revolving metallic ball. From his left palm, he conjured a soldering burn, which wafted into the galactic airspace. He was mesmerising to look at, but too gruesome to stare at for any length of human time. His long, angled face was framed with thick, silky, grey, straight hair that draped onto to his bony shoulders. His head was an oval shape, upon which his two, large, almond-shaped eyes sat bright and alert, with a third eye, appearing as an aperture, placed in the centre of his head. This was his third eye. It was the all-seeing eye of foresight and of the past, and it was closed. His skin was smooth, and even though he appeared wise, he did not appear old. It was only for his grey hair that would suggest he was old. The creature turned slightly to glance towards Amber, and as he did so, James could see that he did not possess any ears. All that was visible were two small, empty holes together with two large, folded, transparent wings protruding from the back of his shoulders. The wings displayed a thick vein as if thick vines growing from an oak tree were rooting from the ground. The wings, although closed, were strong as they swathed down his bony but firm muscular frame. Perched on his left shoulder was a small, red-scaled dragon with a long, spiky tail wrapped and draped around his slender neck like a snare. The scaly creature appeared cute until he opened his jaw. The creature let out a menacing snarl towards James and Amber, displaying his deathly, toothsome mount of daggers, all sharp and fierce in his open mouth with his pertinent, slithering tongue set in a resting place. Ezekiel wore a brown cloth robe falling to the ground. Around his waist, he brandished a glittering, jewel-encrusted scabbard as if he were a solider ready to go to battle, robust and sturdy.

His feet were almost hidden below the magical,

wafting cloak. He stood proud, pounding the ground like a warrior.

Ezekiel hovered, elevated from the ground as a mystical mist surrounded him.

"How do you know my name? Who are you?" queried a beleaguered James.

"I am Ezekiel. I belong to the Secret Alliance from the Sacred Mountain of Truth, where the Thirteen Sages roam free," he said proudly and reassuringly, as if he were reciting from a script.

After a slight pause, Ezekiel said, "Your brother awaits you."

James quickly jumped and became startled, his eyes suddenly opened up wide and alert.

"And my mother? Do you know if my mother is alive?" James questioned eagerly.

Amber glared at James, not really knowing what to do. In her shock, she followed reluctantly, holding her rucksack closely and watching the red, small dragon perched over Ezekiel's shoulder, gawking at her with a menacing stare.

"You must come with me. I will explain. You must always expect the unexpected, Prince James!"

James frowned and quietly followed the strange, obscure-looking Ezekiel.

Ezekiel led the way through the arid land and

through the light source. But as he followed, a small army of strong centaurs and soldiers dressed for battle suddenly appeared, marching and stomping the ground behind him.

James and Amber turned around and watched the strange army following Ezekiel. The strange army marched while crunching and munching the ground with their large, bare feet and hooves. Their elongated, thin fingers clutched their swords proudly. They all followed the gnarled path curiously behind Ezekiel. Amber stared at the ground and grimaced as she saw the twisted path like a spider's web. The dead cranks lay entwined in lifeless vines buried into the ground. Unexpectedly, hideous creatures would spurt out randomly from the cragged rocks, startling Amber. Ezekiel confronted the creatures in a language unbeknown to both James or Amber, and so Ezekiel, with his sword, commenced on a small but tumultuous battle. Ezekiel shouted to his army to assist as they proceeded, whilst James and Amber took refuge between the boulders strewn across the tor. They scowled, having to watch as Ezekiel's army slashed the hideous creatures with their deadly weapons. They were the guardians of the Sacred Mountain, keeping the creatures of the land free and now both Amber and James safe.

They all continued to march, but the red-golden

dragon was still fixated with watching Amber. It peered hawkeyed continuously, absorbed on her every move. Ezekiel bellowed, "The Prince of Oblivionarna coming forth, watch out, stand back."

Unpredictably, a large nebula of bright, luminous, fiery flames exploded, and Ezekiel's army drew their swords as if to commence battle again, but were held back due to the ferocious furnace. Then raging orange and blue flames transformed into a menacing image of evil. He appeared like a gargantuan tower, hovering above all in the galactic airspace, as it turned a burning red. The strange character spat out his orange and yellow fire flames, elevating into the air. He was wafting and swaying his rage in anger towards James.

The fire creature glared down at an alarmed and bewildered James, who was trying hard to supress his fear. "Who are you? What do you want?"

Amber glared as she fixed her stare at the abhorrent fire creature.

"My mother has passed and my brother was left here on the planet. I seek their return!"

"No, no, your mother is still alive. I sent my Minotaur to abduct her. You see, James, I too have powers like you!" The creature roared, as he opened his large hands, bathing in the burning ferocious, bright yellow and orange flames.

"She is now with me in the underworld!" he said, as he let out a menacing snarl and grinned, displaying his deathly wrath. Ezekiel's army, still branding their swords, stood back from the roaring, fierce flames, unable to assist.

Unexpectedly, through the fires, the wild, flame-covered creature lunged forward, spanning his thick, muscular arms wide open intimidatingly, only to display a hologram image of James's mother held in a small ball of fire. His menacing smirk raged through the orange, yellow, and blue iridescent flames.

"Son, take care of yourself. I will see you soon!" Lindiarna spoke gently and peered intently towards him. James was locked in a hypnotic stare, glaring back, wanting to say so much and reach out to her, but was unable to. The heat was too intense, and the temperature was like the Sol Aureus itself! Suddenly, the fire creature raised his arm and pulled over a shroud of lambent flames whilst smirking and throwing his rage towards James. The fire creature continued intimidating Ezekiel, together with his army, trying to hide the fireball holding James's mother from view.

"So, James, if you want your mother back, you must renounce your throne! Simple!" The fire creature boomed his eerie message, leaving a menacing cackle and then disappearing into a bright flash of light, just

Zoran, a solider of Morkann, the demon queen.

as quick as he appeared, letting out a witch's wail. As the creature disappeared, a lingering, pungent smell of toxic sulphur oxide smothered the space around.

James tried to cover his eyes, protecting them from the heat. Amber quickly shot back behind Ezekiel. A distraught James turned to Amber in despair. Ezekiel glared at both James and Amber.

"Prince James, do not be afraid. Come, like I said, *'Always expect the unexpected.'* Your mother is alive, Prince James, and so is your brother. We must travel to the Sacred Mountain as quick as we are able to. We will all be safe there," suggested Ezekiel.

"So, tell me, who was that creature covered in flames?" asked Amber bravely.

"That was Zoran, a solider of Morkann, the demon queen." Ezekiel smiled gingerly. "You are a Carbonite, and our land is different from yours. It will be difficult for you to understand."

"Yes. You could say that, but not so much. We still have weird creatures living on Earth, too!" Amber said, whilst looking at James.

Ezekiel smiled.

"You mean he is a Morkannis?" blurted Amber, referring to Morkann's army.

"No! He is not. He is Zoran! An evil spirit from Moradiya. He lives at the Tower of Belle 'a Noir! Where there is no light and no windows, only darkness! I will help you, but you must imperatively accept as the regent of Oblivionarna. Only then will I be able to relinquish my power to help you, but you must imperatively accept!" Ezekiel ordered, whilst staring deeply at James. His red, scaly dragon again sneered towards Amber with a malicious stare. Amber glared back at the monstrous dragon, who seemed to have a sudden dislike towards her.

She made a face, pulling her eyes inwards towards the dragon, then she stuck out her tongue and grimaced, clutching her Jet-Pack closer. She turned around to make sure James was behind her and trudged on through the gnarled, pitted ground, trying to keep up with the army.

Amber still glared at the small, scaly dragon perched on Ezekiel's shoulder.

"That dragon does not like me!" she blurted, silently hoping someone would hear her.

She continued trekking through the ground, carrying her Jet-Pack over her shoulder.

The dragon's tail slithered from side to side over Ezekiel's shoulder. Amber was mesmerised at the dragon's sudden movements, watching him closely.

"Amber, all you Carbonites have consumed most of the planet Earth's minerals. All of them! There is nothing much left in the cavern, and you must know, located four hundred Earth miles beneath planet Earth's crust, this body of water is locked up in a blue mineral called *ringwoodite* that lies in the transition zone of hot rock between Earth's surface and the core. However, you must note, dear Carbonite, this water is not in a form familiar to you — it's neither liquid, ice, nor vapor. The Sol Aureus has given all it can, and now you Carbonites struggle! You are all a race searching for new entities to explore!" Ezekiel hollered in consternation.

James peered at the army, watching the graceful centaurs trot alongside the soldiers behind Ezekiel. However, Ezekiel was distraught as he gawped at James.

"You must realise, you Carbonites have damaged planet Earth so much. Perhaps more than you realise!"

"What do you mean?" quizzed Amber.

"So much of King Neptune's amphibians from the salubrious shoals have been destroyed. Mmm, you Carbonites have fed hydrocarbons with chemical compounds, which you create. You use them and then feed King Neptune's amphibians, and they are losing their life, drowning in pain and suffering. The ice belt has gone, melting away through the mists. The tectonic plate along planet Earth's meridian line has been changed. The Carbonites have and are still giving out so much damage. Planet Earth's core did consist of a solid inner core and a fluid outer core. The fluid contains iron, which, as it moves, generates planet Earth's magnetic field. The crust and upper mantle form lithosphere, which is broken up into several plates that float on top of hot molten mantle below. Alas, you Carbonites disturb or destroy everything! This has made the spirit of King Neptune so angry. His wrath is unsustainable! You must know that many thunderous torrents, tsunamis, and storms have now been created with heavy hurricanes to follow. Some have happened already on planet Earth. They will swamp to warn, but alas, to no avail. The problem is, many more will come, dear Carbonite, and there will be much more strife." Ezekiel wearily warned and walked on, and his face dropped, as he pointed to the treacherous path in front, covered with rocks and broken, fallen stars, shimmering like jewels.

Amber and James, still holding their rucksacks containing their Jet-Packs, gazed up to see bright, flashing stars zoom past at great speed. They were shining brightly in the black sky around. They watched in trepidation the moving of stars dancing in the black space to form a plough.

"So, what will happen?" Amber questioned anxiously.

"Dear Carbonite, out of the darkness will always

come the light. There is nothing much left. The generous Sol Aureus has given all it can, and now you Carbonites struggle! You are all beings searching for new entities to explore! You must watch this!" Ezekiel ordered, stopping his army from going forward. He then opened his third eye whilst closing his other two eyes. The space above was clear, and Ezekiel's army stood still as they watched their leader click open his third eye like a shutter in a camera. A sudden, luminous, bright orange light beamed from Ezekiel's aperture eye, revealing a screen of past and future events in the life of James. Amber and James glared in amazement as they watched Ezekiel's third eye reveal life before his brother was left on the planet. James was able to view the projection of his brother Tom when they were in their home on planet Earth, happy and carefree. Then the image swiftly switched to show Tom on the burning volcano, scrambling onto the ledge, with his arm and hand stretched out, calling for James through the flames, being held by Natalya, the princess of goodness and light. James glared at the images as Amber gawked on, trying to comprehend the extent of James's loss and grief.

✢ ✢ ✢

Ezekiel's dragon ready to transform into
a gargantuan dragon.

CHAPTER VII

THE REVEAL

It had been some time, and Amber was tiring. "Do we still have far to go?" she questioned anxiously.

James stopped walking and gawked at Amber. A blind rage like a fire swept over him. He was in turmoil with his thoughts of seeing his brother again and perhaps even his mother alive. So many unanswered questions darted through his mind.

"Amber, I really have no idea. I have just been ordered by Zoran, that fire spirit, to renounce my throne! How do you think I feel? Something I can't do!" James rubbed his hand over his forehead in anguish. "If I want to see my mother or brother again, I dread I might have to!"

"Yes, sorry, James, do you think your mother is still

alive? I am just saying, James, maybe what we saw in Zoran's hand was a hologram, an image of wanting to see something that really is not there," Amber retorted, trying to calm James.

"You are right, Amber, do you think it was a mirage?" queried James.

"Perhaps," replied Amber wearily.

Ezekiel could sense both Carbonites were beginning an inquisitive debate.

"Look ahead, over and beyond the ranges and where the cascading nectar flows. You will see the Sacred White Mountain!" Ezekiel said, pointing to a vast, celestial, white mountain peak of spires, which appeared like the icing of a grand cake. James gaped, mesmerised by the image. It was as if a door were suddenly left ajar into some unseen world. They stood in awe as the great mountain loomed before them. They were cold, grey, spikey crevices holding the blood of many battles. While the lower passes wore a cloak of ice, the peaks were crowned with a headdress of ice. Without a word passing between James and Amber, their hearts knew it to be a sacred place as it stilled their minds.

James took a deep breath and fluttered his eyes wide open so that he could feel the rays of Sol Aureus nudge away his captives in the image he was seeing. He realised all of yesterday's mistakes had been forgotten, sensing that he would perhaps be reunited with his family and that his quest had begun.

Amber, still in bewilderment at what was unfolding before her, glanced all around, including the small, red-golden dragon on Ezekiel's shoulder. She noticed Ezekiel was handling the dragon and freeing him from his shoulder with care. The red-golden dragon was deceptively strong. The dragon then opened his majestic, bronze, scaly wings, covered with diamond-shaped scales all symmetrically shimmering in the starlight. His scales were as cold as ice that blazed brightly as an ever-flickering flame. In his chest, he held a hearth of burning fire, although in his remorseless heart lay rime. His menacing, slanted, red eyes could turn anyone who dared to gaze at him into a sickly, pallor shade of fright. His claws held sharp talons and were able to lacerate even the sturdiest of flesh and bone to mere ribbons. His blood was so black that night held an intense radiance that could blind your eyes. His nostrils could smell Amber's dread, and his tongue could taste James's fear. The small dragon, had transformed into a gargantuan monster dragon, held a wisdom like no other and yet expressed a toxic greed. The creature stretched his vast, bat-like wings, spanning so wide that a shadow of blackness was created with its transformation to a huge, ferocious, monster. His multi-chromatic skin, all shiny and scaly, shimmered in the nebula sky. Amber and James stepped back, almost tripping over the mottled, broken stars on the ground. The little dragon did not remain small, but instead had inflated and grown into a ginormous, flying, fire-breathing, ferocious, scary creature. The red-golden dragon was fierce and appeared dangerous when he opened his mouth and yawned, displaying sharply pronounced razor-point daggers shining brightly, and his menacing, slithering, slimy tongue searched for his next meal. He gawped at Amber with his slanted, piercing red eyes.

"I always knew there was something weird about that dragon!" snapped Amber.

"Come, he will take us into the Sacred Mountain, where the Secret Alliance of Thirteen Sages are! We will be safe there," Ezekiel said, pointing with his long, slender finger, gesturing to embark onto the dangerous dragon's back.

The dragon was fierce and had lost its initial appeal. It stared at Amber and roared a loud and tumultuous roar. His diamond eyes were a vile red with fury, and his vapours were full of heat and rage.

"Do you think I am going to sit on that huge monster of a dragon?" Amber moaned furiously with a screwed-up face.

"Amber, come on. Look, right now we have no

Ezekiel's dragon transforms into a menacing, flying creature to take James and Amber to the Sacred Mountain.

choice!" reasoned James.

Ezekiel sensed that Amber and James were nervous about embarking on the now enormous dragon.

"Come, do not be afraid, there is nothing to fear but fear itself! You are from the Carbon world, you have a tendency to fear too much! Do not be afraid. Defeating evil was not going to be easy. There will be times when you may feel powerless. You may look at what is happening or is going to happen, James, and feel scared. You must remember, in darkness all it takes is one match to light up the whole room. Don't let fear take root in your heart. Instead, confront it, no matter how frightening it seems. Don't allow hate or fear to win. You are Carbonites, you need guidance on these planets."

Ezekiel had given the signal and the scaly, red-golden dragon knelt down, bowing his large, scaly head subserviently so that both Amber and James were able to mount onto his back to be seated. James gazed higher and higher up at the mammoth-sized, red-golden dragon, realising the dragon was going to fly them into the valley.

After a few moments, they climbed onto the dragon's back. It felt hard and leathery, and it was covered with hot, cascading, burnt red-orange scales. As they sat on his thick back, Amber and James could see his claws gripping the ground with his long, thick, pointed talons. His back felt like metal, yet it was burning and throbbing in strength with his ever-powerful muscular limbs. They could see his large, scaly chest rise up and down and hear his heavy breathing through his nostrils, releasing heated puffs of red smoke.

The red-golden dragon had transformed into a creature of a phoenix, taking flight at speed into the galactic, infinite space, mesmerising skyline towards the Sacred Mountain of the Thirteen Sages.

Amber gazed around in sheer disbelief, only wanting to record her encounters, when a sudden, blue light illuminated her face. She quickly raised her arms, covering her eyes with her hands to protect them from the bright glare. James had settled onto the dragon's back, knowing that his adventure was beginning and perhaps he would soon be reunited with his brother and his mother. As the dragon zoomed across the planet, James and Amber could clearly view the mouth of the mountain in the distance. They passed through the heavens, supernovas, and galaxies exploding into their vision with endless colours and energy radiating off them, so close to their warm skin. The heat was immense, yet their bodies embraced its beauty and power. James could sense the pulse of the energy coursing through his veins. *This had to be it!* He thought. The mountain awaited as a bright blue sapphire, sparkling light from its carved mouth that illuminated the entrance.

The dragon had fulfilled its cause as it glided through the air. Ezekiel and his army followed, pounding the ground. Then Ezekiel shook his staff, conjuring a puff of mystic green smog to waft over the path.

James stared at the White Mountain, which appeared like a wondrous window of hope. Its glacier icicles formed like spires set on a gothic cathedral in front of him.

The dragon began to slowly descend towards the natural, carved mouth of the mountain, its eyes shaded with heavy rock to form a deep brow. The rocks had fallen to create what looked like high cheekbones with a long, strong, Roman nose and wide-open mouth, allowing the blue, incandescent light to beam through. It was blinding. Amber gazed in trepidation, yet still perplexed and in awe of the new discovery. The dragon landed, facing the bright light with Ezekiel and his army of strange creatures following behind. The dragon descended so that James and Amber were able to clamber off onto the ground.

"You are here," Ezekiel stated.

Amber peered in amazement at the scene in front of her. She glared at the rugged path as James asked in apprehension, "So, I go through there?" He pointed to the mouth of the mountain.

Amber blurted, "Can we use our Jet-Packs to enter the mountain?"

Ezekiel became angry and shouted, "No! You must walk through. You will need to if you are to succeed in your quest!"

Both Amber and James gawped at each other, locking their eyes in disbelief.

"Okay, so we just trek through?" questioned James in total exasperation.

"Yes. You will find everyone you are in search of through there," answered Ezekiel, pointing to the illuminated carved mountain entrance.

They began to walk in trepidation towards the Sacred Mountain, following the bright light beaming through. The mountainous, carved rock formed a humongous mouth as if to receive its meal. It was an eerie sight.

Amber trudged on cautiously, "Great, my boots are so completely ruined! James, and it's all your fault!" moaned Amber, stepping on a broken star, as it evaporated into stardust, illuminating the space above.

"When we get home, I am going to send you the bill! You do know that, don't you?" Amber said in anguish, continuing her sarcastic moan.

They approached the mouth of the mountain precariously, stepping onto fragmented rocks whilst balancing

The carved mouth formed by rock formations.

through the fallen stars scattered in their route. The face of the mountain was huge. It beckoned them to walk further as it illuminated their path. They walked on cautiously, unaware of what was to unravel before them. The glacier was on the verge of a land of ice and snow and stood majestically where the frozen canyons were shaped from engraved rock formations. It was cold and unforgiving. It had become a more treacherous path where they would have to walk.

Amber, completely stunned and bemused as to what was happening, looked up all around her. She tipped her head back, missing a dazzling, shooting star zoom past her at high speed.

"Wow, James, really, this is just so amazing! You never mentioned any of this! I wish I had known earlier, I could have carried out a study on how to meet aliens or how to visit an alien world, or a hitchhiker's guide to new planets and frontiers. What do you think?"

He looked up and pursed his lips at Amber. In the horizon, the light was crystal clear. The treacherous, rugged path in front was dotted with fallen star remnants and rocks. They would have to follow this path, knowing the light that shone would lead him through into the mouth of the mountain.

Then, as if in a dream, a mysterious spectre rose from the darkness around. A brilliant light emanating from its golden, splendiferous orb shone through the gargantuan, open-carved mouth of the mountain. This was all James needed as a sure sign something magnificent was about to be revealed.

His heart began to race like a thousand gazelles in the anticipation of perhaps seeing his family again. The questions he held began to dart around his mind in a complex whirl. Turning to his friend, he said, "Amber, you are a scientist and are always looking for logical reasons to verify anything and everything. But, sometimes, just sometimes, we have to look beyond the pale. There are no answers and no logic. Einstein once wrote, 'Logic will get you from A to B, but your imagination will get you everywhere!' So, perhaps, we have to use our imagination. I did say Astral Dimension, maybe that's it. Absoluteness and nothingness are something to be defined and discovered. Einstein is not me, nor am I him, but it doesn't take a genius to speculate on the possibilities of the great, infinite spacious sea that is our universe. These planets could have been discovered a long time ago, but they were not. Why not? Maybe we didn't use our imagination, just logic! Amber, you see, you must remember, we may not be alone in this universe. But in our separate ways on planet Earth, we *are* all alone."

James paused, as if he had spoken a sermon, then he

continued, "Space is a wondrous reality. With each beat of our dissipating hearts, passages to untouched places are paved. We're not bound by this world, nor are we bound by fear. Nothing binds us to anything, Amber!"

Amber became silent and astonished as she gazed at her friend. Dipping her eyebrows over her glasses in a deep frown, she began to realise his pain in his quest to find his family.

She turned to James, gazing at him. "James, you know I am your friend, and I have a very curious mind. We don't have be the leaf atop of the water, but the penny at the bottom of the pool. Curiosity will always seek the penny."

CHAPTER VIII

THE REUNION

James and Amber reluctantly trudged on, pivoting over the dry, icy, jagged rocks and fallen space debris. The mountain path grew wide where the soil was soft, and then it narrowed, covered with broken stars along its path. There were times it was barely there at all, no more than a mild disturbance in the dirt. But always it led towards the opening of the peak. This was the only destination the two of them could keep in mind. The mountain path was laden with loose rock, each one washed smooth by the ice that once ran freely over them. James braced his feet, attempting to guard against the inevitable rolling in random directions, but his ankles tumbled and rolled left and right regardless. The ever-present cold and vast blackness was their nemesis. For every step forward, they slipped backwards almost as much.

James tilted his head up and saw the path fade into a void of mist and bare twigs. Every third step or so, Amber slipped just a little and righted herself before gravity took her down to the hard-baked ground. "Ouch!" she shouted, her face crumpled into her scarf.

Thick, dark green boughs arched over the path from each side, competing for the light. Under their dappled shade, the harshness of the bright stars was muted, but it did little to make the steep incline any easier. James lifted his eyes to the distance ahead and turned to his friend. "Amber, are you okay?"

Amber took a deep breath, stopping herself from saying anything that might upset James. She realised that this was a quest he had to solve. So, she nodded silently. The path continued, guided by the luminous light, and for a few moments, it simply meandered out of view. James and Amber cared little about the wet mud that now stuck to their boots and their heavy rucksacks that dug into their shoulders. The craggy, grey rock face beckoned with the glow of the blue light illuminating their path, swallowing up the entrance as they got closer.

The strange land was filled with an ominous, brittle silence, but they still wandered on, briskly striding amidst the glistening, musical notes of a serenade emanating out of nothing. They had enrobed the brimless, sparkling pool of infinite space. The hallowed pool of subtle light had adorned itself with the diamonds of countless moons and of a thousand dreams, which once shattered, would explode into short, sharp fireballs, for these wove themselves on a kaleidoscope of cosmic divinity, all hung in the frame of a galaxy beyond human, Carbonite thoughts.

They took gigantic leaps to traverse out of the path which, though it had concealed itself, was occasionally failing to bask in its glory. Mesmerized by their new surroundings, they drifted ahead in the absolute, vast pool of what felt like some unknown divine creation.

They neared the craggy, carved, rock mouth opening, with its ominous eyes glaring at whoever or whatever dared enter its realm. The light became stronger, and their faces became incandescent, illuminated by the sheer light. Both James and Amber raised their hands quickly to protect their squinted eyes.

They proceeded to enter the mountain, adjusting their rucksacks and walking cautiously inside. It was like a giant igloo and seemed to spill into an infinite space of bright, white light adorned with space-dust vapour sparkling everywhere.

"You've done it, James! You've done it!" Amber

exclaimed excitedly, her voice echoing in the empty space.

James was silent and in shock as his stomach flip-flopped. His anticipation of seeing his brother again raised his pulse, and he was full to the brim, trying to contain his emotions. He glanced around inside the pristine mountain. It was entirely soulless, with a bright and clear light, which adorned the cold, glacier ceiling. It was such an enchanting combination, resembling an old castle. It defied belief, growing like a crystal, sparkling just the same as any cut diamond, rising out of nothing to tower above them, only to disappear into a freezing vapour. It was a windowless perfection set in an unknown world. They continued to walk precariously on the silver ground. It felt like it would crack beneath their feet. It was glowing and very bright, in fact, almost luminous. James gazed all around him, at every lurking corner, wishing in anticipation he could see someone, anyone. But to no avail. Amber walked closely behind, shivering. The cold that had seemed mild at first now numbed her face and extremities. What residual heat James had absorbed initially had also now vanished. It had been his buffer, but unwittingly, he had squandered it, believing his thick jacket and boots were enough to preserve his body heat. With each breath, more heat rose in puffs of white vapor, with more heat dissipating into the whiteness, and with each step, the rocks and ice pulled more heat away from his marrow. Amber, too, began to turn a different shade of pale. She quivered through her scarf and coat. Her feet had frozen through her boots, and she stiffly walked on, using her glass spear to launch each step.

She tucked her chin in to her chest to make herself warmer, her teeth chattering. All the while she fervently tried to wish away the ice that clung to her wrapped blue scarf.

"Amber, you must be freezing. We should see something soon, I am sure of it," James said, trying to reassure her.

But Amber had become too cold to retaliate. They both walked on cautiously through the barren, hostile igloo inside the mountain. The igloo was barren and crisp and icy in the same way as a fresh page is white in a new book.

Through the sultry silence, a silver slice of electric light emerged, striking the mountain from inside. Amber, who now resembled a ghost, with her purple lips and chattering teeth, wrapped her coat tighter, pulling her blue scarf around her. She was trembling and cold, nearly frozen. She gazed up through her scarf, and her glasses almost slipped down her face. James and Amber watched intently as the light scattered in the dustless air hovering around inside the vast bowl of still-ness containing their meandering path. The interstellar space they now found themselves in appeared more stark, crisp, and sterile and was lethally cold. A strange creature languished inside the mountain crevice. It peered, then hid away. It took a few steps, causing the soft, powdery snow to gently churn away until it started to rumble down the side of the mountain in a rage, as it plunged down into a crescendo of powder, leaving in its wake a calm pile of snow. Then, a humungous crea-ture intermittently paused to gaze about. Its huge, gla-cier eyes gawked, staring, then disappeared quickly, only to reappear again.

"Did you see that?" questioned an anxious, fright-ened Amber, her voice quivering half with fear and half with cold.

"Yes! Come on, we can't stay here!" James retorted.

They both rushed as fast as they were able to, but they were alone, following a creature or something they knew nothing of, and they were tiring and quivering. Suddenly, Amber, trying to compose herself, stopped. She was too cold to continue. Then, just as James turned to face her, everything ceased. The gentle cascad-ing of snowflakes from the inside of the mountain sub-sided.

"Stop, James, where are we going?" questioned

Amber, who seemed to have sunk back into her sarcastic self.

James came to a sudden halt and turned around slowly.

"I don't know, but I—" At that very moment, the ice from the snow-clad incline stirred. Sheets of ice fell sporadically, like glass shattering. It tumbled from the ceiling inside the mountain gradient, falling onto the glacier inside. They both became startled, standing still, frozen like statues, not knowing where to hide. The snow continued to rumble. The soft snow, emulating icing sugar, covered everything like a winter blanket moving at a slow pace, then a crescendo occurred, and from it, a colossal, mountainous snow wolf. He too was heavily clad in white powdery snow, like a costume. The wolf was fused as part of the snow, except for his eyes, which stood out like rocks that were large, wide, bright orbs the colour of ice, crisp and transparent as icicles. His muscular body and limbs stood towering in the plateau, causing a huge shadow in grey to appear. The creature stood smouldering, wearing an elaborate dream catcher. It was made with beads and gemstones, which glistened like diamonds, flickering from the light onto the white feathers, all dangling from a connected rope from its gigantic neck. He was huge. A giant. Its fur was white, the colour of arctic snow. It was like a blanket, rich, soft, and thick, radiating warmth. There was nowhere to hide, and Amber, for the first time, became petrified. Her eyes frowned, and her mouth drooped. But she was too cold to say anything, frozen in fear. She became a statue. The creature opened his jaw and the points of the daggers inside looked like a cage. They sparkled, illuminating a sense of hunger, as it dribbled. His tongue was pink and fleshy, and it had sagged to one side of his homogamous jaw, as if waiting for a scent or movement for it to make its move so it could indulge in a feast. But the wolf appeared noble and stood still, staring at James and Amber, as if he was waiting for his master.

The snow tumbled slowly, and out of the flurry, emerged a towering figure. She was like an apparition. A siren of light. Her skin was like porcelain and she was surrounded by a white glow. She emanated the entrance to heaven itself, if there were such a place! She was tall, thin and too beautiful to look at. She was so fragile, like glass emulating the essence of the soft, sleepy, snow. Her hair was the colour of golden stars, a shower full of glittering diamonds all swathing, long, silky locks, as if the stars were dancing through her hair, as it gently cascaded onto the ground. Her eyes were crisp, bright, and alluring — spellbinding. They were a rapturous shade of cerulean blue. They held a coruscate gleam

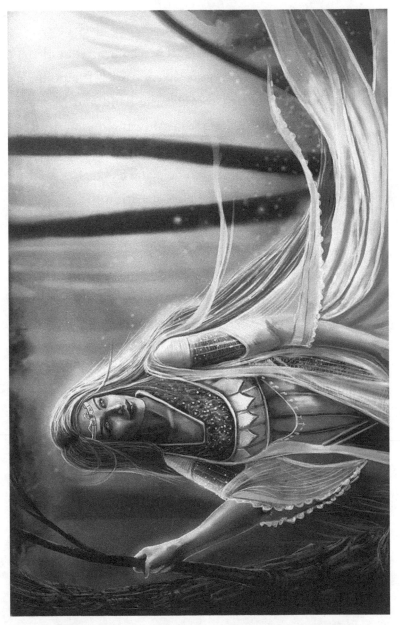

Nataliya standing inside the Sacred Mountain.

that enhanced their beauty. She wore a silver crown, which ran across her forehead. It was an ornate, beaded band, with triangular points, like a castle. The points from the castle darted through the band and in the middle sat a dazzling blue stone. It was a mesmerising diamond, sparkling as an andromeda star. Her long, white, silky gown appeared to float and elevate her from the ground. She was like an apparition. There was something inherently good about her, and James could feel it.

She stood next to the majestic, giant, snow wolf. The creature glared at both James and Amber, but as he gawked, Nataliya glided like a statuesque figure next to the subservient, white, guardian wolf.

Amber, stunned and frozen in awe of what was in front of her, gawked in disbelief. James gave a soft smile. He knew instantly who the statuesque creature was.

"Nataliya!" he blurted.

"Yes, James, it is I." She smiled. "I am pleased you have returned. We have been waiting for you. Come, I will lead you to your brother."

James and Amber gazed at each other for a split second. They stood peering at the tall, elegant, statuesque figure. She was alluring and unforgettable, radiating bright light around her as she glided with her giant, snow-clad wolf dangling his beaded dream catcher and standing proudly beside her. A flurry of soft snow billowed in their wake. Her long, flowing, white, silk gown swayed gently within the cave as they wandered through. She turned to face James, who gave a very pensive look. He and Amber were in complete awe of Nataliya.

"We will go from here. It is a short distance. Come!" Nataliya said, pointing to the meandering path in front.

James and Amber followed her pensively. It was cold, unforgiving, and bleak with a plunging temperature, which seemed to be getting colder in the remote, arctic cave. The air was biting as it spewed out cold, wafting vapour with every step they took. Amber pulled her scarf tighter around her neck whilst glaring at Nataliya and the white, giant wolf following.

"So, are you a friend of James?" Amber asked Nataliya gingerly.

Nataliya gave a long gaze to Amber, radiating a warm smile.

"I am Nataliya, the Light of the Labyrinth! I am here to protect and guide you. When your search is complete, you shall return to planet Earth."

Amber gulped and turned quickly to face James. "Tell me, who is she and do you know her?"

James pursed his lips, glaring at Amber, wishing she

had not asked him to explain anything.

"Amber, let me tell you. She helped me and Tom. She was there at the end, you know, when we were separated on the gorge. She is from a world of subsistence living for all but the mighty who guard their kingdoms from the evil Morkann. She is good! She is able to detect any ultra-negative force with precision. That includes Morkann and her army!"

Amber glared further at Nataliya.

"Amber, don't worry, I know she will reunite me with Tom."

"And your mother too, right?" Amber said, completing his sentence whilst creasing her eyebrows and giving a stern glare.

"Yes, of course," James answered, hesitating, unsure if he would see his mother again.

They continued sauntering on the silvery, glacier-glass ground cautiously.

After a short while, they approached a large, ice opening. "This is where you will see your brother, James," Nataliya said, pointing to the large, ice-clad, narrow opening.

Just as Nataliya had finished pointing to the narrow entrance, a shadow slumbered across the white, transparent ice. James gawked, fixated at what he was looking at. He turned to Amber. He fluttered his eyes, blinking quickly. In the distance, through the soft, emotionless vapour, he could see a tall figure. His heart pounded like a stampede of elephants and raced like a thousand leopards. It was imminent he would see his brother again. His senses all raged, trying to explode. He was too elated. No longer did he feel cold. James could sense it, feel it, so much so that his stomach did a flip-flop. Amber turned to face James, watching his every move as she twitched her nose and raised her glasses back into position. She was still cold and shivering like a leaf, but James was not. He could feel something was about to happen. Amber was bewildered. She used her mouth to pull her scarf up from around her neck towards her lips, taking it into her mouth. James ambled into the narrow, glacier opening to get a good look. The shadow became clearer. It was his brother Tom. He was standing tall. He looked well and strong. James blinked several times, just to make sure it was who he was seeing. Then a wide, broad smile erupted on his face. James released his rucksack from his shoulders, dropping it to the ground. So many thoughts, questions, and answers all jumbled up, like a puzzle darting through his mind. This was it. It was Tom. He was back, and he was alive! James ambled closer and closer to embrace his brother. His heart raced, and his anxiety etched upon his crumpled face like a lost soul.

Tom stood like a prince, proud and strong in his rich, glittering robes and adorned with a glorious, coruscate crown. As they embraced, James realised his search was over.

Review Requested:
If you loved this book, would you please provide a
review at Amazon.com?